In memory of

Mary and Phyllis Scullion

&

Bob Le Galloudec

The Wrackful Tenancy

Charles Dobson

Published in 2020 by YBZcoy
Hyndland Road, Glasgow

Book design by Lumphanan Press
www.lumphananpress.co.uk

Cover design by Claire Adams.

Printed & bound by Imprint Digital, UK.

ISBN: 978-1-8380669-0-1

Extracts quoted from:

The Quiet American, Graham Greene. Penguin Books.

Journey of the Magi, T S Eliot. In *Poets' Quair*, ed by Rintoul and Skinner. Oliver and Boyd.

Tunes of Glory, James Kennaway. Canongate.

A Man for all Seasons, Robert Bolt. Heinemann Educational Books.

The Prime of Miss Jean Brodie, Muriel Spark. The Folio Society.

Scotland 1941, Edwin Muir. In *The New Penguin Book of Scottish Verse*. Penguin.

Dedicated to those teachers, past, present and to come, committed to the advancement of learning by nurturing and maturing the human mind.

Contents

Recess: The Beginning

As usual Barclay stopped in the supermarket to buy something for his tea. A fixed routine.

The interview with Mr Cameron just over an hour earlier had been fraught and alarming. Something appetising, a lasagne and even some wine would be welcomed this evening merely to cheer him up. He bought a mince round, half for this evening, the other half for Thursday night.

On approaching the close entrance, he was greeted by one of his neighbours coming out with his two sons; all three bedecked in the colours of one of Glasgow's famous football teams. He could not understand why a grown man, an educated man, a lawyer, would dress in a football shirt

'Hi, Ian. Boys and me are aff tae the gemme.' Not his usual accent. 'Big European night!'

'Good evening, Mister Cairns. Football tonight?' Immediately feeling foolish, his neighbour was not going to the sheriff court though no doubt some of his fellow supporters would appear there the next morning.

'Told you. It's "Tony".'

'Right,' Barclay mumbled as he entered the close. His flat was on the first floor on the right, two bedrooms, a living room and a dining kitchen; the flats on the left having three bedrooms because the four-storey red sandstone tenement was on a corner. The Cairns family lived on the top floor left. He enjoyed living in the busy, cosmopolitan West End of Glasgow though it was an insular life for him.

The living room, or front room as his mother used to call it, was sparsely furnished with a sofa against the wall opposite the gas-fire set in an old-fashioned metal fire surround, a low, worn but comfortable armchair in front of a low, square coffee table always littered with newspapers, magazines and books, and to the right a small, oval wine table at the right height for his glass of whisky or wine. In the corner next to the bay window diagonally opposite the door, a television sat in a bespoke TV cabinet and in the other corner of the bay, the second armchair. Two dining chairs completed the furnishing. His bedroom was austere with a double bed, a small table lamp centring each of two bedside cabinets, a wooden double wardrobe and the fourth dining chair. The second bedroom was his study-cum-library accommodating a captain's desk with a green cushioned swivel chair positioned between the desk and the large windows, standing along the wall to the right, three expensive, tall, mahogany bookcases, sated with hardbacks, paperbacks and journals, and along the left wall to the door a long coffee table sandwiched between two, low, rounded brown cushioned chairs.

This had been his temple to work but more importantly to knowledge and learning. There were now few papers on his desk and coffee table. A desolated place, visited most evenings before dinner to select the evening's reading either a novel, play or an anthology of poetry. His selected choice was taken to the living room and placed on the wine table beside the evening's chosen drink. Rarely did he read any new literature being content to revisit his favoured plays, prose and poetry: Shakespeare, Webster, Bertolt Brecht and Robert Bolt; Graham Greene, Charles Dickens, Charlotte Brontë , James

Kennaway and Muriel Spark; Milton, Donne, Scott, Blake, Owen, Tennyson and Eliot. Occasionally he would watch television if there was a particular programme which might interest him.

The cooking and eating was routine: sitting in the one chair at the dining table eating the heated half of the mince round sprinkled with some brown sauce, two slices of dry bread, a cup of tea whilst listening to the BBC Radio news. After washing the dishes and preparing the table for his breakfast – the same cup, saucer, tea spoon and side-plate with knife together with another teaspoon and eggcup – he withdrew to the living room.

The first sip of whisky was sharp. The European game was on television and for a moment he considered watching it. Mr Cairns, Tony, would have been surprised that Ian watched football, even more surprised that he like it and other sports. Albeit football was a sport only, entertainment for a short period but not to be discussed and argued over *ad infinitum*. Passion even anger could be vented still on whether England's goal in the 1966 World Cup Final had crossed the line.

It was not important, not as important as addressing the evils of hunger and disease caused by poverty, certainly not a matter of conscience as faced by Sir Thomas More. This evening, he had not expected, even wanted Thomas More to be in the armchair by the bay window, the witness box. In the film of Robert Bolt's play *A Man for all Seasons*, he did not fault Paul Schofield's portrayal of More because the former's quivering head, stony stares and pauses conveyed gravitas. It was better when his guest, his interlocutory or more a witness, had not been portrayed in a play, television or a film. He preferred when the man or woman came from the words not the image. Some he could not take seriously, having no evidential value such as Maggie Smith's Jean Brodie in the film version or Alex Guinness's George Smiley in the BBC television adaptation of Le Carré's *Tinker Tailor Soldier Spy*: the former he felt would ramble on so much without saying anything and the latter would say nothing.

Thomas Cromwell or Richard Rich had not appeared yet. In particular, he wanted the Duke of Norfolk in the armchair witness box in order to justify his lack of support for his putative friend Thomas. But, it was only Thomas that night remaining as ever resolute that he was right to follow his conscience even at the cost of his life. Barclay revered him but could not be like him: he craved More's righteousness. By now, Barclay had downed two whiskies from the Waterford glass tumbler, the Colleen cut. Decisions on his life had been made mostly by others and lamely he had accepted these decisions with the least resistance.

The following day, the branch manager Mr Cameron inquired after his health because he thought Barclay had been a little unsteady on his feet recently. The older man said he probably had more wine than usual the previous night. Another word of caution: Mr Cameron knew he was not a heavy drinker but knew of people especially of his age, unmarried who descended into too much drinking because of a lack of companionship. Barclay snapped that he had his books. Better companions than a partner. He knew it was the whisky which had emboldened him. A puzzled, wary look by Cameron; next, in a friendly tone he said, 'Of course. But be on your guard. In our changing corporate climate, alcohol is potentially career stopping. The company wants to project a moral, clean image.'

Lying to and stealing from clients were acceptable. An unsaid thought. Barclay was not that emboldened.

Barclay had gone to the cinema, watched television or read poetry for eight nights following Mr Cameron's warning and implied threat. After dinner each evening, he had contented himself with two cups of coffee. The branch secretary had informed him that he had seven days holidays remaining and the days could not be carried over into the following year. He considered going away. He had not been to Europe for two years. Previously, especially when he was teaching, he made a number of short trips to Paris, Rome, Vienna, Florence and Amsterdam, spending his time visiting museums, churches, simply wandering, enjoying the food and wine or sometimes beer but always reading. The trips had stopped because of his unhappiness, growing despair with his current employment predominately with Mr Cameron. For others, joylessness in work was a motivation for going on holiday though for Barclay the opposite applied. The constant griping and sniping by Mr Cameron about the quality of his work and his failure to move with the times, was intended to diminish the quality of his life. His manager knew probably because Barclay himself had mentioned it to him that he had to be content at work, knowing he was doing a good job in order to be content in his private life. He concluded that it was a deliberate tactic on Mr Cameron's part with the aim to drive him out.

Tonight, his battered copy of Graham Greene's *The Quiet American* together with a glass of white wine sat on the table to his right. Barclay was reluctant to drink because it could be a difficult night and he needed a clear head, nevertheless he took a minute sip before fixing his attention on the man in the 'witness' armchair.

'Mister Fowler.' Should he call him Tom? There was no response. 'Mister Fowler, why did you murder Pyle?'

'Not guilty.'

'You know that is a lie. What had this quiet American done wrong?' He was determined to remain calm in concert with being analytical with penetrating questions.

No answer.

'You killed him because he was taking your girl... Phoung... away from you.' An accusation not a question.

'You can't really believe I killed him for jealousy.'

'I know you gave the police details of your movements that night.'

Silence.

'What was his name... the policeman... Vigot?'

Silence

'French policeman. Probably not efficient?' Barclay adopted a friendly tone.

'French methods are a little old-fashioned... they believe in the conscience... the sense of guilt... a criminal should be... confronted with his crime... he may break down...' The witness was trying to recall the exact words, *'...betray himself.'*

'Even if you didn't actually murder him, you arranged it?'

Silence.

'Was it because he was an American? You were jealous of him?'

Silence.

The guilty seldom answer questions. His neighbour Tony Cairns had told him that he advised his clients that when questioned by the police to say nothing except 'no comment'. On the few occasions he had been in the lawyer's presence, he felt he was receiving a mini-course on criminal law. He wondered who had been Fowler's lawyer even though he did not recall one being involved.

'You hated Americans! What did you say about...

Granger... *as ill-designed as the Statue of Liberty and...*' Barclay realised he had to check his notes. Surely, this elegant English actor could not be a murderer. Michael Redgrave had been Barnes Wallis in the film *The Dambusters* albeit bouncing bombs had caused the death of many people. 'He saved your life!' He was shouting. Having consumed three glasses of wine, he realised that he was losing his focus. Tiredness was creeping over him: sleep was necessary before he continued the interrogation.

School Pupil

Awaiting his fate, he sat outside the headmaster's office in the full glare of pupils and teachers going up or down the wide stairs. Resisting the tears was difficult.

The first day of secondary school had not proceeded as he expected nor as had been explained in the letter to his mother. The new pupils were to be at school by ten o'clock so that the returning pupils would be in their classrooms. On arrival they had been formed up in the playground in order to be assigned to their classes and thereafter their form masters would take them to their classrooms. There were two other pupils from his primary school, one a tall boy whose mother was a teacher. They had never been friends although they had been in the same class since the beginning of their schooling. The other boy also not a friend did not want to be there preferring to have gone to the junior secondary to be with his pals, and more importantly to be able to leave school at 15 so he could get a job. His parents had other ambitions for their son. The first names read out were for class 1A, the top class. The teacher's son's name not unexpectedly was on this class roll. Barclay experienced a twinge of disappointment because their qualifying results had been similar though he suspected his primary school teacher favoured the teacher's son. More disappointment followed when Barclay was not included in 1B especially when it included the reluctant pupil, well behind him in the test results. His mother would not be pleased.

Barclay was the only pupil left in the playground or the yard as the master in charge of first year called it.

'What's your name?' the teacher asked.

'Ian Barclay, sir.' The teacher spent time looking through the class lists as did the tall, black haired, bespectacled lady who had her own copy of the class lists. She looked severe. He shook his head several times. 'I can't find his name. Can you, Miss Strachan?' The senior school secretary confirmed that Barclay's name was not on her lists.

The solitary, new pupil was despatched to sit outside the headmaster's office to await his fate. He was in his brand new school blazer, white shirt and school tie, short grey trousers, school socks and even new black shoes. His mother had worked extra hours to be able to buy her only son's secondary school uniform. How would he explain to his mother that there was not a place for him at this established school. He hoped that his mother could return the uniform and get her money back. Also he would have to go to the junior secondary, and most of his primary school classmates would laugh at him but not Paul who had cried when he was told that he had to go to the junior secondary school. He would have one friend. But it was his mother who would be upset. There were just the two of them: his father had left a long time ago and his older sister was working in a big London store, Bourne and Hollingsworth, though they heard from neither.

Miss Strachan entered and left the headmaster's office on a number of occasions each time giving him a severe look. He must have done something wrong. He fidgeted with his cap. On the last occasion leaving the office, she smiled at him, saying, 'Don't worry. It's going to be alright. The headmaster wants to see you.'

Mr Cope, the headmaster, was a small, slight man seated behind his desk. He told Ian to sit down. Once he was in the chair opposite the headmaster, Ian could barely see him. In a mellifluous, English accent almost a whisper, the headmaster explained that there had been a mix-up in that they had not received the application from his primary school. However, he had spoken to Mr Cassidy his primary school headmaster who had informed Mr Cope that Barclay's name was at the top of the list but it was not on the list received by the secondary school. Mr Cope explained that it was a mistake, a misunderstanding, no one to blame. The matter had now been resolved and he would be placed in class 1F, the bottom class which was unfortunate considering his test mark nevertheless it was the only option.

'I am sure you will move up after the December examinations. Resilience, Barclay. That is what you need.'

'Yes, sir.' He did not know the meaning of resilience. He was told to go downstairs to Miss Strachan's office and she would take him to his class.

'Remember, Barclay. *Resilience*!'

His secondary education had proceeded without any further drama. He worked hard in class, did his homework and achieved good marks in the term exams thereby as predicted by the headmaster moving up to near the top class. Extracurricular activities did not hold any interest for him. Memberships of the debating and chess clubs were short-lived. Barclay did not make any close friends nor did he make any enemies, never feeling that he had ever been bullied unlike primary school. Sometimes on a Saturday he would go with some of his fellow pupils to the pictures or the cinema as called by the more sophisticated pupils. He never expressed a preference for any particular picture, simply agreeing with the majority. Barclay liked films, finding contentment in the cinema though siding with the majority view in their post-film discussions. He continued to go to the cinema but preferred to be on his own.

His mother still working hard was pleased with his school reports. Also, his mother seemed less worried which was no doubt because his sister was back in contact, had visited a couple of times and was training to be a nurse though still in London.

English literature was his favourite subject. His fourth year English teacher, the principal of the English Department, was responsible for transforming it from a favourite subject into a passion. The principal, Mr Baxter, sat in the high-backed, wooden, teacher's chair, his legs usually crossed, reading to and discussing with them plays and poems. During their year with the principal they had read only one novel, a Dickens. Mr Baxter seldom stood up or used the blackboard. Plays and poetry were about the spoken not the written word.

Was it morally right to assassinate Julius Caesar for the good of the republic and the people? *Et tu Brute* was now a term of condemnation signifying the most heinous act of treachery. Or had Brutus been traduced unfairly? What were the meaning and limits of friendships? Was Mark Anthony an opportunist, a spiv? How could Mr Baxter use a term to describe a common conman, a cheat, for the heroic Anthony! Indeed, their teacher used it immediately after he had read, no, recited with passion Anthony's oration: '*Friends, Romans, countrymen, lend me your ears; I come to bury Caesar, not to praise him. The evil that men do lives after them, The good is oft interred with their bones; So let it be with Caesar*'

Disquiet and dismay was the reaction in the class. Surely, Mr Baxter was not going doolally. *He was old!* His two hands rubbing from hip to knee his right leg which was crossed over his left leg, he was silent for almost a minute. He spoke quietly, 'Young men, in a few years you are going to leave behind the comfort and security of this institution. You are going into a world which can be hostile and corrupt. No doubt most of you will go into the professions even teaching.' A wry smile. 'You will have to make decisions. Judge people. I don't mean you will have to decide if someone is a murderer – though for those who go into law, it might become a possibility. You will face dilemmas. You will be required to make decisions.' He paused and scanned the class. 'Are you making a decision for the right reason? Does it help or harm people? I am sure you will all make the right decisions. What about others? Are their decisions right… honest? Cause harm to others? Not stealing from others… especially from those who are less well-off.' Another pause. 'Literature is not just for our enjoyment… which it is most certainly. But we study plays, poems, novels in order to hone your judgment skills.' He looked round the class, a fleeting gaze for each pupil. 'We hope that you will make wise and moral judgments.'

Mr Baxter declared that his mission was challenging them to think beyond their years and maturity.

In fourth year, the only discordant note came from the young, laconic history teacher. During a lesson on the causes of the French Revolution, he pronounced that they, the pupils, did not own the literary texts which they read, merely renting them in the same way Shakespeare had borrowed history to write plays like *Julius Caesar*. They had no proprietary rights to literature, but, they did have ownership of their own history which they themselves could shape just like the sansculottes. The history teacher asserted that Marx and Hegel understood the dominance of history. Barclay had heard of the former but not the latter. He wished he had chosen geography. It was rumoured that senior pupils had complained of the history master's teaching in that he debunked accepted facts of history such as Britain standing alone in 1940 against Hitler. Moreover, he was an anti-royalist and affirmed it was better red than dead. On the causes of war, several times whilst teaching he had declared, 'Conflict is caused by loyalty to land and ideology.'

A classmate whose father was a teacher in the school stated confidently that the history teacher would not last long. He was right!

It was in Robert Bolt's play, *A Man for all Seasons*, that the young Barclay found his hero, Sir Thomas More, executed by Henry VIII because he refused to swear an oath on the validity of Henry's marriage to Anne Boleyn. For Barclay, More had made a moral judgment but arguably not a wise one.

Barclay's passion for literature was sealed by T S Eliot's *Journey of the Magi*. Immediately, he identified his life with the first few lines:

A cold coming we had of it,
Just the worst time of the year
For a journey, and such a long journey…

He thought he would need to give some more consideration to the poem's final line:

I should be glad of another death.

At this moment in this year of discovery and exploration, death was the furthest thing from his mind.

Thanks to the teaching by and encouragement from most of the teachers, he obtained a place at university.

University Student

University for Barclay despite what the lecturers said at the start of each term was a continuation of school except he did not wear a uniform, though a uniform of sorts: jeans, shirt, pullover, sometimes a jacket. He attended every lecture and tutorial, always making copious notes and his essays were always in on time. Similarly as at school he had no friends but was friendly with most of the people on the same course. It was strange to have girls in the class, still, they were friendly and bright. His social life was limited though initially he went to both Unions being separate male and female ones. Occasionally, he attended the Friday debates in the Men's Union but became bored with the preening, aspiring politicians – the future Mark Anthonys.

Uni or stretched by the Glasgow accent to "the Yoonie" became the centre of his life. He felt happy and secure there. The Yoonie was a comfort blanket. He spent as much time there as possible delaying having to return to his mother's home in Reidvale Street in the East End of Glasgow.

In his first year tutorial group, the tall, English boy was confident and amusing, always willing to contribute to the discussions even though Barclay thought most of his contributions were shallow and contentious. Eventually, he realised that Peter Mayne was stirring matters deliberately to make the tutorials more lively and fun. Some tutors appreciated Mayne's contributions, others took the opposite view. In tutorials the same three students, two males and one female, disagreed, fought, consistently and heatedly with Mayne's opinions with the Belfast girl particularly being more vociferous and aggressive, nevertheless tempered by an impish smile. Sometimes, to deflate those impressed by Mayne's arguments and extensive knowledge, Bernadette, or Bernie, as she preferred, quipped, 'He says more than his prayers, that boy.' Notwithstanding that Barclay had never heard of the expression, he thought it was a wonderful way to suggest someone was exaggerating possibly even lying though he felt that accusation could never be made against the English student. Yes, he could be verbose at times. In the heated, tutorial battles, more often than not, Mayne won the neutrals round by being reasonable in understanding other points of view, and also by being self-deprecating. Mayne had the same routine *ante-* and *post-bellum,* coffee with two or three girls from the tutorial group.

After one tutorial, having an hour to wait for his next lecture, Barclay went for coffee. Seated alone at a corner table, he was reviewing his tutorial notes, deleting the points which were not relevant and underlining the salient ones.

'Hello, Ian. May I join you?' Barclay recognised the voice without looking up. Mayne sat down without waiting for an answer. 'Thought I would give them a miss today.' Giving the girls a wave and a smile. 'It's good for them. Keeps them interested – unless you want to join us?'

'No, no. Just trying to sort out my notes from the tutorial.'

'You want to try giving that a miss sometimes.' Mayne grinned. 'More coffee breaks. A few beers sometimes.'

'I suppose you are right.'

'What's your name again? It's Ian…'

'Barclay.'

'You don't own the bank? ' Another grin.

'Bank?' A confused then comprehending pause. 'Right. Heard of them. Don't think we have them up here – maybe in Edinburgh.'

'So you're not rich. Just another impoverished Scot!' He responded quickly to Barclay's surly expression. 'Joking.'

'Right. You do a lot of that.'

'Joking?' A nod and a smile. 'Only way to keep me sane here – apart from the girls.' He changed the subject. 'You know what I like about you?' A quizzical expression from Barclay. 'Your independence. You are self-contained.' Barclay thought he was being mocked. 'Everyone else needs friends, mates but not you. Some of the girls like you because of it. You're mysterious. They have decided that you have a girlfriend who is not here at uni.' A surprised look. 'No, no. I haven't been sent over to find out or fix you up with one of them.' Mayne's head gesturing towards the three girls. 'I wouldn't do that… anyway want them for myself. I'm greedy.' Mayne turned serious. 'You know what I admire you for? Well two things.'

Barclay thought again he was being mocked. 'For?'

'You don't say much but when you do, it's always on the button. I take a note of what you say… to use in the exams. Also what Bernie says.'

'The Belfast girl?'

'Yes. She's clever.'

'Don't think she likes you.'

'Another accurate insight by you. But I like her – and I think she likes me – a little. But I'm working on it.'

'What about the other two – Paul and…'

'You mean Pinky and Perky.' A vigorous shake of his head. 'Just trying to impress Bernie. Hoping to – never mind. They are buffoons – eejits!' He smiled. 'I like that word. Never heard it before I came to Glasgow. It's really good for describing – eejits.' Both laughed. 'The other thing is your ability to quote from books and plays. I know we have all memorised poems… but you can remember large chunks of the texts. How do you do it?'

Barclay shook his head. 'I don't know.'

'That could be very useful to some people. Could get you a job.'

Peter Mayne came from a large, Catholic, Anglo-Irish family who lived in Pendleton near to Manchester. Originally the family name had been Kelly-Mayne but the 'Kelly' had been dropped due to its connection with Ned Kelly, the Australian outlaw mythologised in the song *The Wild Colonial Boy*, and because Peter's grandfather wanted to conceal their Irish Catholic roots for business purposes. Mayne told Barclay that he was unsure whether the former was true but undoubtedly the latter was true. Most of his many siblings, all older than him, had set up outposts in different parts of the United Kingdom. One of his brothers was in his final year at Oxford. 'In contrast,' said Mayne, 'I am slumming it here at Glasgow.' Barclay knew, or hoped, the Englishman was joking.

Barclay's social life improved, in fact started, thanks to Mayne. They would have coffee together a couple of times a week. Sometimes, Mayne joined him when Barclay was having his pre-packed lunch usually on the same bench at the front of the main building overlooking Kelvingrove Art Gallery and the Kelvinhall in which carnivals and exhibitions like the Ideal Homes were held. Beyond were grey, dismal tenements and work yards many billowing pungent fumes. Sitting on the lunch bench, now and again Mayne would observe, 'It's such a dreary and grey place.' Barclay turned down Mayne's offers to treat him to lunch in the refectory.

At least once a week they would go to the Union or a nearby pub for a couple of beers. Sometimes on these occasions, girls, Peter's girls, would accompany the two boys. Barclay enjoyed talking to the girls, in particular to Gillian, yearning to have a closer relationship with her. He did not ask Gillian out due to fear of rejection. In the Union, there were usually other guys at their table but Mayne never invited these or any other guys to the pub. Barclay felt more at ease without other males there, and thought it was deliberate on Mayne's part. On almost every occasion, Barclay apologised that he could not go with them to a dance in one of the Unions or somewhere else, or to a party in someone's flat. He had to go home because his mother was home alone, and he needed to study to catch up. On one occasion despite Barclay's protests, Mayne was insistent that they go over to the East End so he could experience the real Glasgow. Peter's girls were unwilling to go but Bernie decided to tag along. Barclay felt compelled to invite them up to his home though his mother was out with his Aunt Hilda. Peter and Bernie were shocked by the small cramped flat which Ian shared with his mother and especially the dinginess of the close though neither disclosed their thoughts. On the Gallowgate, they survived two pubs, in both an air of malevolent hostility saturated the smoky dreariness. The Irish girl and English boy were relieved to escape to the West End.

Barclay's lack of money was never mentioned though it was there like *Banquo's* ghost. Once or twice, Mayne made vague overtures about subbing him but never made an actual offer. For Barclay, an ambivalent relief.

Towards the end of Whitsun term, Mayne told Barclay that he was changing his degree from English to a joint History and Politics degree. Barclay was surprised that Mayne was being allowed to change his degree course. Mayne explained that it was not a problem because he had good A-Levels in both subjects, and their course contents were equivalent to the university's first year. However, it would not impact on their friendship and they would still meet for drinks.

It did!

They met infrequently and usually by accident. Barclay returned to his customary routine and behaviour notwith-standing that on a few occasions, some of the girls from the tutorial group including Bernie persuaded him to go for a drink but could not convince him to go to concerts and other functions. He came close to asking one of the girls out but the right moment never presented itself.

In his second year, Barclay concentrated on his studies seeing but not meeting with Mayne. Meeting for drinks with the girls from his tutorial group dwindled mainly due to them having boyfriends. However, he had a couple of girlfriends which ended quickly because they soon realised that he was diffident and uninteresting. Near to the end of term he began going out with Christine, a Belfast girl also studying English. He had been intrigued by her greyish blonde hair. Her passion was classical music and sometimes she sang in the university choir as well as a local church choir. She had strong opinions and like Belfast Bernie was not reluctant in expressing them so Barclay's quietness was not a barrier to their relationship. Barclay saw her as a prettier more moderate Madame Defarge. He thought he was experiencing love for the first time which was not enclosed in a novel or play. During the summer she was going back home to volunteer for the Northern Irish Civil Rights Association. Even though she was a Protestant, she felt the Roman Catholics had received a raw deal. He was disappointed that on her return after the summer she did not want to go out with him, gravitating towards the politics students though with a wistful gaze she told him that one never knew what the future might bring.

His studies did not suffer. He read and reread the set texts and the recommended texts as well as other works of his own choosing or mentioned by Bernie and others. He became more discerning in his reading selection: the writer's name and reputation were unimportant. Dickens was a superb writer demonstrated by novels like *Great Expectations* and *A Tale of Two Cities* but considered some dross such as *Barnaby Rudge* and *A Christmas Carol*. Similarly, Sir Walter Scott's novels were turgid almost unreadable but thought his poetry such as *Marmion* outstanding and in particular *The Lay of the Last Minstrel*. Of course, this led to disagreements with others which did not escalate into arguments due to Barclay shrugging his shoulders, saying it was only his opinion, not engaging with his opponents to their frustration. Comparisons were made with Mayne who would have argued even if he had not read the disputed text. Probably true!

In May of his third year, Christine told Barclay that Mayne was sharing a flat with Bernie and two others on Hyndland Road near the university. Bernie had invited Christine and her new boyfriend to a party in the flat. Also, Bernie said that Mayne was insistent that they bring Barclay threatening to deny them entry if they didn't bring him. Reluctantly Barclay attended.

The flat was on the top floor. The rectangular hall was almost as large as his mother's two room and kitchen flat on

Reidvale Street. The party was in the hall and dining kitchen which was more than sufficient space. Most of the guests were politics students who had an opinion on everything, vociferously. Barclay felt out-of-place. Mayne had greeted him, said they would chat later but he needed to circulate to look after the guests. After two bottles of beer, Barclay had decided to leave but waited for a chance to tell Mayne.

'Not yet. Let's go into my room.' He had what was the living room with a large bay window providing a superb view of the university tower. Unsurprisingly to Barclay, the room was a bit of a mess. Mayne said that Bernie had the other large room to the front with a biology and a history student renting the two smaller rooms to the rear. No, he was not going out with Bernie but he was still working on it. The politics students were getting excited about the general election in June. 'They are all fucking dickheads!' Barclay thought this was the first time he had heard Mayne swear. 'It doesn't matter whether they are Tory, Labour, Liberal even the few Scot Nats. They have surfaced since Winnie Ewing's election victory in the Hamilton by-election in sixty-seven. Anyway forget those pricks. How are you doing?'

'Fine. Okay.'

'Sorry we haven't been able to get together. Miss our chats.'

Barclay left unsaid, "Not really chats. You talked. I listened."

Mayne was not going on to do Honours. He would be working in the Politics Department assisting one of the professors in analysing the 1970 general election results then writing a paper on his, the professor's conclusions. The expectation was that Labour would be returned albeit with a reduced majority. Wilson even though he was a shit would continue as Prime Minister. Ted Heath, the leader of the Tories, was generally not seen as a credible Prime Minister.

He did not have the common touch. Being a bachelor was another issue which could result in people not voting for him. The British liked their leaders to be part of a solid, family unit. Like the Royal Family. Even if they were all having affairs. Well, except Her Majesty. Mayne remained unwavering in having and expressing his staunch opinions: it was like a part of his body. Barclay had no knowledge of, and no interest in these matters. This would be the first time he had a vote. He would probably vote Labour.

Starting in August, Mayne had a job teaching history in one of Glasgow's private schools which was not alone in taking uncertificated teachers. It would be only for a year, thereafter, it was back down south but probably to London. He had a brother, the Oxford one, and sister working there. 'Why don't you come to London? You will have graduated – sure we could get jobs. My brother would help.' Barclay said not very convincingly that he would think about it but he had to concentrate on getting his degree. Mayne responded with an 'as if that was a problem' look. They agreed they would resume their get-togethers. Outside the two double-doors on the landing, Barclay paused not thinking about going to London but forming an aspiration to have a flat in Glasgow's West End though he would not need one as large as Mayne's.

Barclay's honours year had gone well, being in demand in that some of his peers and third year students sought his advice and assistance for their essays. Bernie said that he should charge them for his time which Barclay considered was not moral or right – the influence of Mr Baxter. Some of his lecturers raised the possibility of him coming back for a PhD though the head of department said not to get ahead of himself, and to wait for the exam results. His social life continued as before with several girlfriends though fizzling out due to the lack of common interests in particular their lack of interest in Barclay's new found love for the writings of the Russian Fyodor Dostoevsky and the German Bertolt Brecht. Bernie cautioned him against reading so much, firmly telling him, 'It will do your head in.' He did not tell her that one of the reasons for reading so much was in order to ease the pain of his loneliness.

Brief greetings were exchanged with Christine when they met though he yearned for a closer relationship with her. He wondered if he loved her but unlike most of his male peers he had no one in whom he could confide. He thought of broaching it with Mayne on the few occasions when they met for a couple of beers, or five or six for the Englishman.

Barclay did not obtain the first-class degree he had hoped for and others had expected, though his mother was delighted by him obtaining a degree, the first ever in the family. Bernie had told Mayne that she thought Barclay had been denied a First because the head of department found him odd and Barclay did *not play the game*. They agreed not to mention their suspicions to Barclay.

His mother, his sister Elaine and his Aunt Hilda, his mother's only and older sister, attended his graduation ceremony. Students and lecturers came over to congratulate him, some expressing surprise that he did not get a First. Bernie's parents could not attend the ceremony and her guests were a cousin who was a nurse in Glasgow and Peter Mayne. Barclay did not see Christine at the graduation. At the post-graduation drinks reception, Bernie and Barclay indulged in mutual congratulations. Tentatively Barclay inquired if she knew why Christine did not attend.

'She's in Belfast trying to get civil rights for us poor, downtrodden taigs – Catholics.' In response to Barclay's puzzled expression. 'Think she's going to do a PhD at Queen's in Belfast.' Followed by a mischievous smile. 'Want me to get a message to her?'

'No no. Just... wondered.' Nervous faltering.

'Right. See you later. Think Mayne is organising food.' She turned away, paused, swivelled her head over her left shoulder back towards Barclay. 'By the way, I'm not from Belfast.'

'Oh. Peter know that?'

'Less he knows the better.' Another mischievous smile as she turned away from him.

Later, Mayne joined Barclay and his guests. After the introductions prolonged by Elaine Barclay's interest in his family, Mayne said, 'Right. I've booked a table for a late lunch.' His usual authoritative tone. 'My treat for our two esteemed graduands. No. Graduates.'

'Oh no, son, we... thanks anyway.' Mrs Barclay was uncomfortable. 'You young ones go and enjoy yerselves.' She turned to her son. 'Your Auntie Hilda and me will just go and get a wee cup of tea somewhere.'

Hilda's face showing disappointment. 'Okay Jean. We'll just go and get a cup of tea.' Through a muted sigh.

'You coming wi us?'

'I am not!' declared Elaine Barclay. 'I am going for lunch.'

'Good,' said Mayne. He glanced at his watch. 'We'll go in twenty minutes or when they stop serving drinks. Good.' He turned away, stopped and turned back. 'By the way, Ian, managed to organise... well my sister did, teaching jobs in a sixth-form college in Kensington. You teaching English, me politics and some history. Start in September but we need to be there by the end of August for admin and stuff.

Accommodation sorted. In my sister's place.' He noticed the disappointment, concern on Mrs Barclay's face. 'We can discuss it at lunch.' It was a deliberate ploy by Mayne to raise it in front of Mrs Barclay. He had mentioned to Barclay several times that at some stage he would have to *break free* from his mother. But Mayne knew that he could not leave it to Barclay to engineer his own freedom. Elaine's response to the lunch offer made Mayne think that she might be a possible ally in persuading Barclay actually Mrs Barclay.

Once Mayne was out of earshot, Mrs Barclay said, 'Kensington. That's down in London.'

'Yes, Mum.'

'Son, not sure if…'

'Mother. *London*. That's where I am living. Remember!' Elaine was exasperated. Mayne's assessment was accurate. 'It's not on the other side of the moon. You have been there.'

'I know… but he's still a wee bit young.'

'Gawd. He's a man. And in Kensington. That's a posh place. Must be a good school. And digs sorted… better than me when I first went down.'

'I know, Elaine. But you were different… you were older.'

"Christsake," was left unsaid. 'A wis sixteen.'Anger accentuated her Glasgow accent. 'You mean a wis harder. A had to be, growing up wi you and ma dad.' She caught Hilda's restraining shake of the head. 'I'm sorry.'

'Jean. It will be good for the boy to get away. He needs to get a job anyway.' Hilda did not know that he did not want a job but had hoped to carry on at university doing a PhD. His ambition to be an academic had been frustrated. 'Anyway, you will not have to work so hard. Sure that Ian will send you some money. They're paid a lot down there.' Hilda knew that Elaine was now sending money to her mother. 'It will give the two of us more time together.' Another incentive. Hilda's husband had been killed in Burma in 1945. She had no children and never remarried. 'We can go to the bingo, the pictures. Even take coach trips. Remember how you always said about going up to the Trossachs and Loch Lomond. We can go to Edinburgh… maybe the Tattoo.'

'Aye, suppose.'

The three women had discussed Ian Barclay's future as if he was not present.

'Oh, Peter's waving us over. Time to go. See you later, Mum.' Elaine was walking, on the cusp of running towards Peter and the two girls.

'I better go, Mum. Sure you will be okay?'

'Yes, Ian. You go and have fun.' He could see tears at the back of her eyes. He hesitated.

'Just go, Ian. I'll look after your mother.'

'Thanks, Aunt Hilda.'

Barclay relaxed and enjoyed the lunch after Elaine had told him that she and Aunt Hilda would work on their mother, and that he *would* go to London. Having Aunt Hilda on his side was good because his mother listened to her. Life was bad enough when their father left but it would have been worse if it had not been for Hilda's support. Hilda wanted her sister to retain her self-respect but they would not have survived financially without Hilda's discreet support. Reluctantly, even after a few wines, Elaine confirmed in response to a question from her brother that she had left home to lessen the financial pressure, allowing their mother to concentrate on bringing up Ian. He was reappraising his sister in that she was not the selfish daughter and sister who did not give a hoot for her family. Nevertheless, he was embarrassed when Elaine asked

Peter if he had an older brother, if not, he might have to do. Bernie said, 'Maybe then, he'll stop pestering me.'

Ian Barclay thought it was the best night of his life... despite not getting a First.

School Teacher: London

The arrangements were completed for the move to London.

Mayne said to Barclay, 'You know it's a Catholic sixth form college.'

'Thought so with the name. Why?'

'Well, up here in Glasgow... well you know better than me the problems with sectarianism. Probably being exacerbated here because of the troubles in Ireland.' Surprisingly, Mayne was more conscious of the sectarian divisions in Glasgow than Barclay. Although Barclay lived in the rough and mainly poor East End of Glasgow, his father originally from Perth was determined not to let religious bigotry infect his family. His mother was not tainted by sectarianism due to the influence of her sister Hilda who was vociferous as well as truculent in opposing it. She had married a Roman Catholic which had brought criticisms from friends and neighbours. She did not conceal her scorn for her critics pointing out that unlike her husband, most of their fathers and husbands were not called up, having secured reserved occupations in the McFadzean factories. Hilda's husband was killed on active service in Burma in 1945.

In Glasgow and the West of Scotland, sectarianism was manifested mainly through football in the form of Celtic and Rangers, the former supported mostly by Catholics and the latter by Protestants. Ian was so inept at football that none of the street teams wanted him. In primary school when the others were playing football or other games, he was content to read a book. Also, despite the Catholics and Protestants attending different schools, he did not see much evidence of conflict, with most of the boys seemingly accepting that they went to different schools but after school and on Saturdays they played football together or games like "kick-the–can".

As far as Ian Barclay could recall the Catholics and Protestants got on reasonably well with each other except for some trouble around the time of Celtic-Rangers football games, called the 'Old Firm', and the Orange Walks. On Sundays almost all of the Catholics boys went to chapel while fewer Protestant boys attended church. After the services, they resumed their football and other games. The games were played in the back-courts of the usually four-storey tenement buildings.

The back-court just called 'the back' was an area for two closes, sometimes one and rarely three. The close was the street level entrance to the stairs which led up to the houses. The back had a place for the rubbish bins: in the poorer parts of Glasgow called the 'midden'. Most backs had a wash-house but by the time Ian Barclay was going to secondary schools, most were not in use and many had been bricked-up. Mothers and daughters hung up the washing on clothes lines in the back. But the back was more than an area to dry clothes.

The back was a colosseum in which great, dramatic events were re-enacted. One day it was filled with the Hampden Roar, the next the politeness of Lords or Wimbledon – though 'good shot' sounded harsher in the aggressive Glasgow accent. The back could transform itself into the Great Plains of the American West; the deserts of North Africa where the British tommies fought the German Afrika Korps; or some far-off jungle where re-incarnations of H Rider Haggard's *Allan Quatermain* searched for lost treasure or re-instated African kings. Likewise on occasions, it was requisitioned as a theatre for singers, a gambling den, a boxing ring and even a gospel hall for itinerant lay preachers.

The young Ian Barclay seldom participated in or watched these events.

Marie-Theresa or just Marie to her friends, Mayne's eldest sister, and a lecturer at University College London, owned a three-storey end-of terrace house in Rochester Square in Camden Town. A friend of her husband-to-be taught at the Catholic sixth form college in Kensington, and had enquired if she knew of any recent, top-grade graduates who might be looking for some teaching experience. They had been in the habit of employing Oxbridge graduates but they tended to leave as soon as they secured a post at a public school thereby causing disruption during term. The college was looking for people who would commit for at least two years.

She was a bit reluctant to recommend her at times. errant brother even though he did have some teaching experience. More persuasively, it would resolve the conundrum of what to do with her house. Following their marriage, she was moving into her husband's house in Muswell Hill. The Rochester Square house had been bought with the support of her family, and the mortgage payments met by renting out rooms to mostly post-graduate students from the School of African and Oriental Studies commonly referred to as SAOS.

On the ground floor, Mayne would have the first room on the left, a large, bay-windowed lounge which had been Marie's room. Ian Barclay would be given the slightly smaller room next to it looking out over the back garden. Both rooms had been converted into en suite. On the first floor were four bedrooms and a large bathroom. On the top floor there were three smaller bedrooms and a shower room. The bedrooms each had a washhand basin. The communal rooms were on the ground floor: a dining room opposite Peter's room with the long kitchen behind it. A pay telephone was fixed to the wall beside the kitchen door with a toilet just before the door into the small garden. All the bedrooms were let at present. The room above Peter's was reserved for Peter's brother, the Oxford graduate, though he lived with his wife in another part of London.

Mayne explained all this to Barclay when he arrived from Glasgow as well as sighing at the Glaswegian's comment about *Jane Eyre* and *Mr Rochester*. Mayne's brother who worked for an investment company in the City used his room to meet clients whom they were trying to steal away from other investment companies. These were high-value clients therefore the need to be discreet to avoid the watching eyes of their present companies. Barclay did not understand this need for secrecy but did when Mayne said, 'Probably also uses it for shagging so his wife won't find out!' His sister didn't mind them having small, drinks parties as long as they finished at a reasonable time in order not to disturb the neighbours. No illegal drugs even cannabis were allowed in the house. This breach of the tenancy would result in immediate eviction; as would bringing prostitutes into the house which was directed mainly at the SAOS overseas students. Peter explained that his sister had high moral standards as a result of her convent school education which Barclay understood. Mayne commented that his experience of convent-educated girls was the opposite which Barclay did not understand at that time.

The young men settled into their teaching careers quickly and relatively easily due to most of the pupils, or students as they were called, being eager and well-motivated. Barclay was surprised by the number of Indian, Pakistani and Chinese students as well as a couple of black boys of West Indian background. His own primary school class had been a white sea of faces, and only one Indian boy at his secondary school. At university there had been Chinese, Indian and Pakistani students though most seemed to do medicine or mathematics. Barclay became popular once the students became used to his accent which he had not realised was quite so pronounced, and he did make a successful effort to soften his guttural Glasgow twang. When he raised it with Mayne who seldom had difficulty understanding Barclay, he said, 'Don't worry. It's *the Londoners*. They don't understand anyone not from London.' He tried to reassure him. 'Your accent's not too bad. It's the Scousers... from Liverpool, the Welsh and the Geordies. And especially people from Birmingham and places like Walsall they don't understand. They might as well have come from darkest Africa.'

Barclay was conscientious and diligent in his teaching. His breadth and knowledge of literature astounded even experienced masters. R. C. Sherriff's play *Journey's End* was the only text he did not know but he mastered quickly the World War 1 set play. He was available even during breaks and lunch-times to assist any student. The first problem arose when a student asked him if he could talk to him about a personal matter concerning another student. Barclay was flummoxed and embarrassed both by the nature of the personal matter, and that he was not much older than the student. He told the student in a stumbling, nervous voice that he did not have time at present but would speak to him later. He sought guidance from Mayne who directed him to the senior master in pastoral matters. Tactfully and quietly the students were informed that

Mr Barclay did not have the necessary pastoral qualifications. Thankfully no student ever approached him again seeking guidance in personal matters.

During the term after his first Christmas, the English Department had a new teacher, not only a female but also a nun, Sister Mary Joseph. He was at a loss how to behave towards her. Again, he sought Mayne's advice which was to invite her out for a drink in the Irish Centre in Camden Town. Stumped momentarily, but realised it was just Mayne being himself. Sister Mary Joseph came from Winchester in Hampshire. She was a strict disciplinarian in class but had a sharp and wicked sense of humour in the staff common room, blaming her father who had been an army officer. Sometimes Barclay called her Sister Helena even Sister Sandy then apologised. After it had happened three or four times, Mary Joseph inquired why. No, she had never read *The Prime of Miss Jean Brodie* though she had heard of it and its author Muriel Spark. She would now. She did and stated that she would like to teach it but not to adolescent boys.

During his time in Rochester Square, Barclay never encountered Mayne's brother, saw any drugs or prostitutes though he was not sure if he would have recognised the latter. Their social life was good and varied though limited for Barclay who had much more preparation and marking to do than his flatmate. One Saturday evening, they went to the Irish Centre a few streets north of Rochester Square. A loud, big, silver-haired Irish priest vetted entry at the main door turning some away. Barclay could not understand what the priest was saying to individuals though he thought the priest shouted at two girls, 'Come back when you are attending Mass again… and don't come here half-naked!' Once they reached the holy doorman, Mayne leaned close to the priest's left ear, both being of similar height and build. Barclay could not hear what his friend was whispering, though it had effect: a thin smile but not sufficient to change the priest's stern expression accompanied by a wave through with his right arm. The three males behind them were less fortunate as they were subjected to an aggressive interrogation.

It was a loud and boisterous atmosphere created by the live music and the conversation. Some people spoke to them and when they realised Barclay was Scottish or Scotch as most of them said, they were keen to find out where he came from, the team he supported and if he might know some of their relatives who lived in Glasgow. The priest transformed into the bouncer, pre-empting possible fights and ejecting individuals, some for aggressive behaviour, others for immoral conduct on the dance floor. The Glaswegian felt uneasy, alarmed, even frightened. He did not go back to the Irish Centre though Mayne was not put off and seemed to thrive on the atmosphere.

Mayne would go out with his brother for a few beers and on his return would tell Barclay about the cracking Irish pubs around King's Cross. He had found a new term, *the craic,* grading pubs by the *craic.* Mayne would tell Barclay that he would take him the next time the two brothers went out on the sauce or the piss. Also, Mayne would sometimes go to his sister's for supper, and for lunch with his two siblings usually on a Sunday. On some occasions, another sibling or two who were visiting or passing through London on the way to Cornwall or Paris were at the lunches. Again, Mayne reported to him that Marie was insistent that Ian should come to supper or lunch. Barclay never went to any pub with the two brothers, nor attended any supper or lunch, and did not meet any of Mayne's many siblings.

His conclusion was Mayne thought that the Glaswegian was

too common, not sophisticated enough for the refined Mayne family. Or possibly, Peter was embarrassed by his siblings, a flaw in the family, his brother was mad. Barclay had heard of highly intelligent and educated individuals descending into madness. He insisted to himself that the lack of invitations did not bother him because Peter was his friend not his family. Though it did peeve him a little.

Elaine Barclay had a self-contained flat in the nursing home which she managed, no longer a matron. Barclay had visited his sister several times though it was a long trek by bus from Camden to Purley, south of London. To her brother, she seemed quite prosperous. Their mother had stayed with Elaine twice during his first year of teaching, now more reconciled with her son being in London. On one visit Barclay and his sister went to her local pub where she knew quite a lot of people. She went to the bar to get the drinks, a half pint of lager for her brother. He was embarrassed when she returned with his lager and a pint of bitter for herself. His admonishment that she should have a glass of wine was met with, 'Piss off. It's London not Glasgow!'

Barclay returned to Glasgow for the summer holidays. Immediately, living in his mother's house made him unsettled and unhappy. His mother was working still but on shorter hours and when not working visited or went out with her sister Hilda. Barclay spent most of his time visiting museums, doing research in the Mitchell, a large reference library, and spending time in the cafes and pubs around Byres Road, the centre of Glasgow's West End and near to the university. He could nurse a coffee or half pint for a considerable time as he read often rereading the school texts, making notes for his lessons. He returned to the flat in Reidvale Street in time for tea with his mother, sometimes with Aunt Hilda present. Twice they went to Hilda's home in Salamanca Street in the Parkhead area of Glasgow. When he was young, he had always liked going to his aunt's house which had been an oasis of calm and order compared to his own house especially when his father lived there. Barclay could not remember his father going with them to Aunt Hilda's. His father had left them in the summer before Barclay went up to secondary school.

When a boy, his visits to Aunt Hilda's had provided comfort and a sense of safety. On Hilda's dining table was set a place for each person: a pictorial or floral place mat, a china cup and saucer, a side plate centred with a knife on a cloth napkin, and the appropriate cutlery depending on what was being served, usually homemade soup with bread. There were cakes and biscuits to accompany the tea after the soup though depending on the time of day it might be just tea and biscuits. On almost every visit before and after his father left, the sisters went into the front room for a wee chat. On their return, Barclay could see his mother had been crying. Elaine had told him that their mother was confiding in her sister about their father's behaviour, and that usually Aunt Hilda gave their mother some money even if it was only a few pounds.

The pride of place on Hilda's mantelpiece was a framed photograph of her late husband in uniform and, leaning against the frame, an envelope addressed to her but at her previous address in Parkhead. In the past, her sister would ask often why she never got married again to be answered with a look at the photograph on the mantelpiece, and a smile. That night which turned out to be the last night he was in his aunt's house, Hilda told his mother that she had arranged a holiday in Arran for both of them and that Ian could go also but he declined. He thought that this was the first time he had realised what a strikingly handsome woman Hilda was even though she was in her sixties and now retired. She was not much taller than his mother but held herself erect, straight-backed in comparison to his mother who appeared small, frail even shrivelled. He understood why. He decided to ask his aunt about her husband. He had never had any interest in soldiers or war but in reading *Journey's End*, he discovered an appreciation for their courage and sense of duty.

She had met Iain, with an 'i', Munro in Edinburgh where she was working in a hotel. He came from Perth though worked in the design office of a Glasgow shipbuilder. He had been visiting his family but stopped off in the hotel for a meal before returning to Glasgow. On informing her that he did not like Glasgow, she responded that was because he did not know the right places to go to. She agreed to show him the right places when she came back to Glasgow on her days off. It was out of character for her as she had been rather pernickety about boys; agreeing nods from her sister. There was just something about him, a calmness, stability and he seemed decent, not rough or brutish. At the time, her family lived in the Dalmarnock district of Glasgow. He rented a room near to his shipyard.

After a short time, she knew that she wanted to marry him. It was not to escape an overcrowded home as she had criticised other girls. The only problem but not for her was that Iain wanted to get married in a Roman Catholic church or chapel as most Glaswegians called an R C church. Eventually they married in the registry office followed a few days later by a church service in a religious house near Perth. Hilda found Iain's parents and his only sister friendly and welcoming.

The recently married couple moved into a two room and kitchen flat on Duke Street close to her current home. When war came in 1939, Iain volunteered immediately for his local regiment, his father having served in it during the First War. To his wife's question of why not the navy, he stated that he did not like ships. He was killed in Burma in 1945 in the last action his unit fought against the Japanese. He was a lieutenant having gained a battlefield commission. The letter was from a brother officer. She would not let Ian read it until after her death, and she would bequeath it to him in her will.

His mother said that Iain Munro was a very good and caring person, which her son interpreted as a rebuke of his father. Her son had been named after Iain Munro but his mother had registered him without the 'i'.

After the war Hilda worked in the Glasgow Central Hotel but took some night classes for typing and secretarial work. About 1951 or 52, she obtained a part-time typing position with Finlayson's, a small metal company. The boss's son returned from the army about a year later with the intention of succeeding his father though he was not interested in the business. When he discovered that she was the widow of Iain Munro, he had insisted that his father give her a full-time job. Once or twice he spoke about Iain, praising him which she considered him simply being kind. When she mentioned the letter from a fellow officer, he said he did not know about that but that particular officer certainly would not have written it if he had not held a high opinion of Iain.

Robbie Finlayson studied accountancy and when he set up his own firm, he employed Hilda as his secretary. She learned to do book-keeping and accounts. Robbie said that she would pass the accountancy exams easily but that would mean losing her. He increased her salary and gave her a bonus at Christmas and in June. Other members of staff were not aware of it and she did not flaunt or brag about her salary. Often, she spent her holidays with her late husband's family in Perthshire. Her one unspoken regret was not having a child, never understanding why she did not become pregnant. She saw the regret in her mother-in-law's eyes though the latter offered the explanation of it being God's will. Hilda's regret was blended with ambivalence in that she was unsure whether she would wish to raise a child, Iain's child, without the father.

When his mother and her sister went on holiday, Barclay booked a seat on the overnight coach to London, his return train ticket fixed for a set date and not being able to afford to buy another train ticket. He was impatient to return to London. Mayne was surprised to see him back early. It was a brief reunion: Mayne was going up to Manchester for a wedding and other family events.

The remaining weeks before the beginning of term, Barclay explored London, taking in the sights including the Tower of London and St Paul's Cathedral, thereafter some of the many and varied museums, and finally just ambling through different areas. Initially he researched the areas that he intended to visit but ditched the planning after a few days opting instead for a bus or tube to take him to an area like Hampstead of which he knew the name, or an area with an interesting name like Elephant and Castle. As in Glasgow, he stopped in cafes or pubs for sustenance. He found most people to be friendly, and well-disposed towards the Scots though most were aware of Glasgow's reputation for violence. Sometimes he found himself returning to the same cafes and pubs because people knew and welcomed him. As in

Glasgow, he went to the cinema usually in Camden Town, or the one on Haverstock Hill in Belsize Park, and occasionally to the famous and expensive ones in and around Leicester Square.

Sipping a glass of wine outside a pub near Regent's Park, he was content and relaxed. The words of the *Duchess of Malfi* resonated: London freed him from the Glasgow cage. London was freedom and equality. Yes, there was still the class system with at the apex, to him, a family full of gormless-looking individuals. But it did not intrude on his life. The people with whom he interacted treated him well and with respect. The college principal had been effusive in his praise for him, even hints of a permanent contract.

Thereafter, for the sole purpose of seeing his mother, he returned to Glasgow at Christmas and for a few days during the summer holidays. He also made a point of meeting his mother when she came down to stay with Elaine, at least twice a year. He was surprised, a little bewildered by how Elaine could pay for these trips.

Barclay and Mayne socialised together less and less. The former did not mind because he was making friends including girls in his own right. Barclay continued to have the heaviest work-load, spending most nights in his room, marking and preparing for lessons. Mayne had invested in a television, and as their rooms were adjacent, its noise sometimes disturbed Barclay. On rare occasions he would ask Mayne to turn down the volume. He did not consider that Mayne was idle and negligent in regard to his teaching. Often his friend had declared that teaching history and politics was easy: he just waffled. But Mayne had a good grasp of both subjects, both being conscious parts of his life. He recounted to Barclay how history and politics, sometimes religion, were discussed during most family meals. Barclay postulated that Mayne was much more intelligent than him. At weekends, Saturday was for wandering, Sunday for marking and preparation.

Mayne had a very active social life though on more and more weekends, he was going home to Manchester or to a sibling's in another part of the country. Mayne and Barclay remained friends and tried to go for a drink with each other at least on one or two Fridays in the month. This was to catch up but Mayne was becoming more and more preoccupied with the situation in Northern Ireland, 'the Troubles'. Barclay was aware of but took no interest in the events in Ireland though it was tending to dominate conversation in the staff common room as a number of the staff, teaching, administration and domestic, were Irish Catholics concerned about their families in the North. At the college Masses, there were prayers said for peace and reconciliation in Ireland though sometimes for other events like the massacre of members of the Israeli Olympic team in Munich. After one Mass, the principal spoke to all members of staff acknowledging the tensions caused by 'the Troubles' but reminding them that their primary responsibility was towards their students. Barclay's Glasgow upbringing made him know not to become involved in the discussions. His routine gave rise to his not spending much time in the staff common room instead remaining in his class in case any of the students needed help.

Just after his second Christmas at the college, Elaine arranged to meet him for lunch in a pub near Victoria station. He could tell that his sister was nervous even anxious which was unusual, leading him to surmise that there must be something wrong with their mother.

'Ian, I need to tell you something but… please keep calm…

don't shout at me.' He was perplexed but was relieved because it was probably not about his mother. She took a sip of wine. 'I have been seeing Dad.' In response to his puzzled expression, 'Dad. Our father.'

'Oh!' His mind was unusually stumped, blank for a few moments. 'Why? Where? Is he in London? Christ he's not here!' He was looking around the pub, searching faces.

His sister smiled. 'He's not here but yes he does live in London.'

'But why?'

'He's my dad. I know what he did to Mum and us was wrong. He didn't care! He was selfish! He caused us all but especially Mum pain and unhappiness. And I told him. I didn't hold back.' It was a prepared speech. A short, silent interlude. 'He would like to meet you.'

'No, no. I can't. Not after what he did… it wouldn't be fair to Mum.'

'Listen. You know the money I used to give Mum and… and her visits down here. He paid for them.'

'I wondered how you could afford it.'

'He's doing alright for himself. In insurance… financial services or something like that. I have managed to put away some money.'

'Elaine.' He was shaking his head, looking down not at his sister. 'It would not be right.'

'Ian, just hear me out. He wants to meet you next Saturday in a restaurant on Haverstock Hill. It's an Italian on the other side from Belsize Park underground. Do you know it?'

'Yea.'

'He'll be there from one o'clock. It's up to you.'

Barclay was unsettled for the rest of the week, debating in his mind, moving from "absolutely not" to a possible "unlikely" then "maybe". He tried to hide his concerns, his angst, from his colleagues, mostly successfully but Sister Mary Joseph on the Thursday asked if everything was alright. She said that she had never seen him so down but if he did not want to confide in her, he should talk to somebody even the genial giant, her slightly barbed, pet name for Mayne. He took her advice.

On the Friday evening when Mayne wanted to go out for a few beers, Barclay suggested a coffee and a wee chat. With their mugs, they settled in the two worn, low armchairs framing the bay window of Mayne's room. Barclay gave his friend a concise family history. He was a good listener, and not as was his wont in conversations interrupting or seeking clarification albeit he was not sure of Barclay's reason for disclosing – what he had always suspected – family strife though that was possibly too strong a word. It became clear when Barclay told him of the prospective meeting with his father.

'Are you going?'

Vigorous shaking of his head accompanied his declaration, 'No, no. I can't… feel as if I was cheating my mother… being disloyal to her. What do you think?'

'Well, Ian, it's a decision only you can make.'

'I know. I know that… but…'

Mayne spoke in a low, soft tone, 'Family conflicts are the most difficult and complex to resolve.' He thought of his many family crises down the years: some even those before he was born were still causing bitterness, anguish and recriminations with uncles, sisters, cousins not speaking to each other. 'What about the principal's urging of forgiveness and reconciliation?' It had been in reference to Ireland.

'I'm not a Catholic. I'm not into forgiveness.'

'It's not just Catholics, all Christians... even Buddhists... I think.'

'I don't believe in God or an afterlife or anything like that!'

'Well, you seem to have made up your mind.' Both men were quiet for a short period. Mayne decided on a different track. 'Thought about the what if? What we call counterfactual history. If you don't go, you might wonder for years what if I had gone. It might nag at you. What is it they say? – It's better to have tried and failed than never to have tried or something like that. I think you should go.'

Barclay was pensive, still torn. 'I'll think about it.'

Donald Barclay was just finishing his lunch having decided that after forty minutes, his son was not coming. His father looked old and worn which gave him some spiteful satisfaction having for some reason anticipated the same young, fresh-faced man of his memory. His father stood up but did not offer his hand. 'Ian. It's good to see you.' A slight nod from his son. 'Sit down.' Once they were both seated. 'Some lunch? Food is good here.' His son would have some bread with olive oil and a glass of white wine. The younger man felt with his stomach churning that he could not eat in case he threw up. Once Ian had put his first piece of bread in his mouth, his father said, 'There's no point in me apologising. It would be a futile gesture. I know I did wrong... that I hurt your mother... and you and Elaine.' No response from the younger Barclay.

That morning when Barclay told him that he was going to Belsize Park, Mayne said, 'Can I give you some advice?' A consenting nod. 'Don't get involved in recriminations or arguing. It won't resolve anything. Listen to what he has to say before you say anything. Might be better if you say nothing but I know that might be difficult. Good luck.'

'We were too young. We were happy at first… but we realised we had nothing in common.'

Ian Barclay remained silent and unconvinced.

'I had been in the air force… been overseas… just couldn't settle when I came back. I tried,' his father said.

His son unconvinced.

'A mate from the air force contacted me about a job… but it would mean coming down here. Your mum was not willing to leave. I just felt that I had to try.' Mayne's counter-factual.

Ian could not recall his mother, Elaine or anyone saying his mum had refused to move south. Simply, he did not believe his father. He was finding it more and more difficult not to challenge his father. His son's silence relaxed Donald Barclay. 'Then we got into selling insurance then property management… and security. We were doing well.' A thin, smug smile.

'You gave Elaine money to help Mum.' A statement.

'Yes. Felt it would help. Just trying to do right.'

' Restitution.' Not a question.

'Son, I just wanted to help'

Ian Barclay was surprised that he remained outwardly calm and in control but he did not like confrontation, being alien to his nature. He was in no doubt that Elaine would not have held back in her criticism of their father.

'Think it's too late for that.' Almost a whisper, avoiding his father's eyes

His father nodded, 'Okay.' He requested and paid the bill. He was known to the waiters. He stood up, slung over his right shoulder a black, airline cabin holdall, at the same time took out a laden brown envelope. He placed it on the table. 'This is for you.'

'No.'

'If you don't want it, give it to charity. Don't put it in the bank. Spend it and you can save your teacher's pay.' His son continued to look at the table. 'It was good to see you again. I hope we can meet again. If you want to, Elaine knows how to get hold of me.' A pause. 'Bye, son.'

Hearing the door open, Ian Barclay glanced round to catch his father leaving, pausing on the pavement, looking left and right, before turning right to go down Haverstock Hill.

He knew he would take the money but wanted a reason, an excuse, to do so. Elaine did not seem to hesitate and indeed went on taking more, but, she had always been hard-headed and pragmatic. She saw it as her due, as restitution.

Later, he recounted the meeting to Mayne but found it hard to recall the actual words and sequence of the encounter. It was not written words.

'Money seems a bit dodgy. What does he do?'

'Selling insurance, property management and security.'

'Probably is dodgy. Cash in hand to avoid tax.'

'I feel like Wormold.'

'Who?'

'*Our Man in Havana.*'

'Yes, of course... But you're not telling lies, cheating the British taxpayer.' He changed tack. 'You know that book made the SIS review its practices on paying agents in case real agents were screwing them.'

'SIS?'

'The Secret Intelligence Service is... I have told you that before!'

'Yes, right.' Barclay was not surprised in that Mayne

seemed to know about such things though was unsure of the credibility or reliability of his knowledge.

'Think of it as alimony.'

'That's for children… or a divorced wife.'

'It's backdated!' Mayne flashed his convincing grin.

'Dad seems to think it went well,' said Elaine.

'He's lying.'

'I know. That's what he does.'

'Elaine, did you have any doubts about taking the money?'

An immediate and decisive retort. 'No! We're entitled to it. Mum, you, me.'

'Are you going to tell Mum?'

'No!'

'You're probably right.'

'I am… and another thing, it's better we get it than the pubs, the horses… or some floozies.' She smiled. He wished that he had his sister's uncomplicated, resolute way. 'Are you going to see him again?'

He shook his head. 'Probably not.'

'His money?'

A tad of hesitation then a confirmatory nod.

'Good. This is for you.' In a fleeting moment, she had taken the envelope from her bag and handed it to her brother.

'Thanks.' Now he would be able to go to the theatre more.

'I'll get your share but don't give any to Mum. I'll sort her.' A conspiratorial smile. 'I'm now her good daughter not that ungrateful wean.'

The interviews for the staff on temporary contracts with the principal were scheduled for the Friday in the penultimate week of the term before the college broke up for the long summer holiday. At these interviews, they would be told whether their contracts were being transferred into a permanent one, the current contract extended or terminated though some would have secured a permanent contract with another school. Unsurprisingly but for no credible reason Barclay was concerned: most of his colleagues expected at the very least the extension of Barclay's temporary contract. The night before the interview, Mayne went into Barclay's room with two mugs of coffee.

'Thanks, Peter.'

'Don't worry. You'll be fine.'

'What time are you in?'

Mayne with a faint smile said, 'I'm not.'

'What!' Barclay was visibly surprised.

'I saw him last week. Told him I was not staying.'

'You didn't.'

'The principal asked me not to tell anyone, to give him time to get somebody. He said if he couldn't get anyone he would give me a permanent contract. It wouldn't have made a difference but agreed not to tell anyone. He's been fair to me… Thomas Yates is a decent guy.'

'Have they got someone?'

'Yes but grateful if you don't say anything till it's announced officially.'

'Right, of course.' A pause. 'Have you found a new school?'

'No. I'm leaving teaching.'

Barclay was stunned. 'What are you going to do?'

His friend explained that he was joining the police or the army having been accepted by both. He had just over a week to decide because the next training intake for both services started on the same day. The principal had agreed he could use the Friday morning for packing up, coming in after lunch to complete the necessary forms and say goodbye. To Barclay's query on how he would manage packing up in one morning, Mayne explained that his sister had organised a van to take his stuff home. Anyway, he had to go back to Manchester on Sunday to speak with his parents who were concerned at this change of career. He could sort out his kit at home. The good news was that Barclay could move into the larger and brighter bay window room, and that Marie would not increase his rent. It was an extra £5 notwithstanding that he had not paid it. A self-satisfied grin. He would leave Barclay his T V set but he had to remember to pay the licence fee. He would be inviting people for a few farewell drinks tomorrow evening. He had hoped to organise a bigger and better farewell but his agreement with the principal had put the kybosh on that.

Barclay's appointment had been moved from the morning to the last slot of the day. The principal was apologetic, uncomfortable. There was no question of not extending his contract. The principal could not be more satisfied with his teaching and commitment especially to the pupils. He was an example to all the staff, no matter their seniority and teaching experience. He had hoped to reward him with a permanent contract but this was not now possible due to unanticipated circumstances, Mr Mayne leaving. A replacement had been found for Mr Mayne, a high quality, experienced master. However, his agreement was conditional on a permanent contract, naturally considering his experience. The principal had only one permanent contract available which he had intended to offer to Barclay but could not now in the circumstances. Even more regrettable, another condition of the new master was to be placed a few points higher on the pay spine, and consequently, the principal did not now have the money to place Barclay higher on the temporary pay scale. He would seek additional funding from the governors but could not promise that additional funds would be forthcoming. He would allow Mr Barclay the weekend to think about it, and in the circumstances, he would certainly understand if he found another post. He could be assured of an excellent reference.

Barclay remained deferential to those in authority and especially to older people. 'Thank you, sir.' Barclay looked at the floor; the image of sitting outside the headmaster's office on his first day of secondary school reeled through his mind. 'I will stay, principal… if you will still have me.'

The principal stood up thrusting out his right hand. 'Thank you, thank you.'

The pub was crowded, boisterous and smoky. Most of the younger members of staff including the secretaries had turned out as well as a few of the more mature staff. Mayne was popular not so much due to his teaching ability as to his sense of humour and a certain charm, or roguishness as described by a rather staid, female, maths teacher. Mayne was in his top effervescent and ebullient form. Other Friday night regulars had been roped into the party, no doubt most knowing Mayne from previous evenings. Barclay having secured a position at the end of the bar, observed the merriment only being interrupted occasionally by brief chats with colleagues, and waves from Mayne accompanied by discreet pointed fingers or hands at females with whom no doubt he hoped to end the evening.

He had two pints of lager. Barclay realised he had consumed almost the whole bottle of white wine placed in front of him after he had finished his second pint. He was disappointed no angry, no bitter, well a mélange of the last two emotions.

Why did Mayne not tell him about leaving? The commitment of confidentiality to the principal was a fig-leaf: Mayne knew that he would not have betrayed his confidence. Further, his action had thwarted Barclay from being given a permanent contract or at least an increase in salary. He finished the last of the wine and feeling unsteady on his feet, decided to go home. He would have it out with Peter Mayne in the morning.

He woke just after eleven in the morning feeling woozy, his mouth thick and sticky, and with a thumping above his right ear. He could not remember how he got home though he was pretty certain that he had used the tube for part of the way and that two young ladies had helped him into a taxi. They knew his name, calling him Mr Barclay. Students possibly? He needed more sleep but needed a drink of water now. Slowly, he raised himself out of the bed managing to reach the wash basin. He realised he was wearing his trousers and shirt even his socks. He let the cold water run for a time – being something he had done since childhood – before filling a glass. He drank the water quickly and refilled the glass. This time he drank slowly whilst looking at his reflection in the mirror, being appalled and knowing his mother would be shocked at the sight. Then Peter Mayne seeped through the fog in his mind. 'Fuck!' A rare expletive from him. He went into the hall. Some of the post grad students were in the dining room having a late breakfast or early lunch. There were some bemused glances at Barclay's dishevelled appearance.

A sign on the door read, 'Ian Barclay's room. Do not enter.' The key was in the lock. He went into the bay windowed room. All evidence and signs of Mayne were gone. The room had been swept and dusted. The bed had been made with new, fresh sheets and pillowslips. There was an envelope addressed to him centred on the desk flush against the wall opposite the door. He closed the bedroom door, sat down at the desk and picked up the unsealed envelope. For a short time, he held the envelope in his right hand, staring at it. Finally he took out the one sheet and read it:

My dearest Ian,

I am sorry that I did not get the opportunity to say goodbye to you and to thank you for your friendship. My sister took control of me moving out. As I told you before I admire you very much. My admiration has grown here in London. In particular, I admire your strong sense of right and wrong, a product of that esteemed, sober Scottish education which is admired throughout the world.

I regret that you did not get a permanent contract. I accept responsibility.

I regret even more that I did not tell you of my intention to leave. The fact is that I did not finally decide until I was in the principal's office. I know that you would not have betrayed a confidence. Please forgive me.

I will let you know where I end up. The coming family council could be difficult.

You can contact me via my sister Marie. If you move, please give your address to Marie.

Take care,

Yours Aye

It was signed Peter Mayne. Followed by:

PS Remember I told you that your prodigious memory could get you a job. Still could happen. Likely my brother or one of his associates will be in contact soon.

He reread the letter several times. He smiled recalling Peter and some of his antics. But the letter also peeved Barclay. He did not think all the words were Mayne's. Did Marie also control the letter writing? The reference to 'family council' bothered him. The thought leapt into his mind that Peter had disgraced himself. A child out of wedlock? The eminent, Catholic Maynes would be appalled, dishonoured. What was the male equivalence of banishing a daughter to a convent?

No. He was being ridiculous, over analysing.

He moved into his new room rearranging the furniture so that the desk was at the bay-window. It would provide more light and a better view as he marked his pupils' work and prepared his lessons. There was more shelving for his books. At least there was an up-side to Mayne leaving; regretting the thought immediately as being a little mean.

On the Monday of the last week of term, with pupils not needing any support, Barclay found himself in the staff common room. There had been some chat on Mayne's farewell but it moved onto the ongoing cricket test match and plans for forthcoming holidays. Barclay did not have a class after the morning break and decided to stay to finish his coffee. He had not yet fully recovered from the previous Friday's over-indulgence. He picked up *The Daily Telegraph* though he seldom read any newspaper.

'Feeling better?' asked the staid, maths teacher as she sat down.

'Oh. Not really. Not used to it. Miss…' trying to recall her name.

'Miss Amato. Veronica. We are colleagues. We can use our Christian names in here.' She gave him a cheery smile. 'Get home alright?'

'Yes though…' He closed over the paper, laid it on the

coffee table and recounted the story of being helped by two kind girls who seemed to know his name.

'Of course, they did.' The smile had erupted into laughter. 'It was Trish – one of the secretaries – and me.'

' I am sorry. I didn't realise.'

'We saw you going into… staggering into the station and thought you might need some help. Didn't realise that we live close to each other.'

'I'm sorry.' The colour in his face conveyed his embarrassment.

'Ian.' A cheeky smile. 'May I call you Ian?'

'Yes. Of course.' He thought for a moment. 'Did you pay for the taxi?' A confirmatory nod. 'I will pay you back. I'll get you some flowers, chocolates.' Blushing again. That was what was expected in thanking a lady. 'For both of you.'

'You can get chocolates for Trish. I'll settle for a drink. After the principal's drinks party on Friday afternoon, we can go to a quiet little pub I know which is close to your place.'

'Not sure.' Hesitant, thinking of a reason not to, then he smiled. 'Yes. I would like that.'

'You're buying.' A playful smile. 'And don't forget the taxi fare!'

Life was good, interesting and especially rewarding for Barclay. He continued to enjoy teaching, never becoming blasé about his skills. He had inherited Mr Baxter's mission: challenging his students to think beyond their years and maturity. His exploration of London continued sometimes returning to the same areas. Also, he ventured beyond the capital to Canterbury, Winchester and Salisbury, being impressed by each city's great cathedral; less so with their surviving, allegedly medieval buildings. His father via Elaine continued to provide him with money. He had met or bumped into his father on two occasions resulting in brief chats which included the son declining invitations to lunch. His sister Elaine suspected that these were engineered chance meetings. She continued to meet with her father once every four to six weeks in order to ensure the money flowed. She continued to berate him for his past conduct, and told him there were to be no more chance meetings with Ian. There were none. Barclay was surprised that their father tolerated Elaine's treatment of him.

'I think he puts up with it because he is desperate for some human contact with his family.'

'Do you feel sorry for him?'

'No… well possibly a wee bit now. He's a broken man.'

'He brought it on himself.'

'Hilda. Aunt Hilda.' In response to her brother's disapproving expression. 'She thinks Mum could have been maybe a bit more understanding… tolerant of his behaviour, his moods. She said the war changed some men. She would never know whether her Iain would have been different. He didn't come back so he remained perfect.'

'What did Mum say?'

'She didn't say it in front of Mum.'

Veronica Amato was his first long-term, steady girlfriend. Her family had been interned at the beginning of the war because of their Italian origins. Later, her father and his brother, her uncle, had served in the Forces, one in the Royal Engineers, the other the Royal Navy. Her family had a cousin in Glasgow who owned an ice-cream shop but Barclay did not know it. Veronica was determined to get a teaching job overseas, in a military or international school in somewhere like Singapore or Hong Kong. They both should go because the money was good and the lifestyle was much better than the UK according to a friend who was teaching in Singapore. Barclay said that he was settled and happy in London; anyway, he had moved down from Glasgow. This assertion of an equivalence between Glasgow to London with London to Singapore or Hong Kong brought teasing of him for a while.

At the end of the school session the following summer, Veronica had secured a post in a Catholic school in Singapore. Despite her best efforts and encouragement from other colleagues, Barclay would not go. Indeed, Veronica's future school wrote to him offering him the post of assistant head of the English Department, and most likely head of department when the current holder retired at Christmas. He declined. He was settled and happy in the Kensington College. One colleague explained that the college for Barclay was like a well-worn pair of slippers, or a favourite pair of corduroys and cotton twill shirt, only to be met with a riposte from another colleague that Ian Barclay most likely had never worn and was never likely to wear such clothes.

Also in the same period, his sister was leaving her boring job to return to Glasgow. Their Aunt Hilda was not able to look after herself and intended to go into a nursing home. Elaine would take control of vetting the nursing home because some of these homes were scams and not fit for pigs. She would manage Hilda's affairs because her aunt told her that Elaine's mother was not up to it. However, she intended to return to London as soon as possible. Ian Barclay's sole concern was the continuation of his father's largesse which was essential for his lifestyle thereby allowing him to save a little. An exasperated Elaine told him not to worry as she had made the necessary arrangements with her father.

Barclay did not return to Glasgow that summer despite Elaine speaking of the need for an extra pair of hands. Instead, he took himself off to Europe with an interrail pass, visiting Heidelberg, Rome, Florence, Vienna, Berlin, Amsterdam and Paris. He travelled by ferry, mostly train and sometimes by bus. He treated it as recompense for Veronica, and even Elaine, deserting him.

In Vienna he had met a girl, Irmelin, in a bar on Schonlatergasse. It was frequented by students and professors from the nearby art college as well as self-styled poets. The girl had spoken to him. She wanted to practise her English. She was tall, with blonde hair, stunningly beautiful. Barclay could not understand why she would speak to him but she insisted she had to improve her English which was perfect already. With the flexibility of his interrail pass, he decided to extend his stay in Vienna. Each day after visiting the city sights and museums, he ended up in the Schonlatergasse bar. Irmelin was always there different from the girls at home, exotic even. In what was to be his last meeting with Irmelin, after a few beers he declared his love for her. She was apologetic and empathetic. She was going to London to be with her future husband. She had not been leading him on but simply wanted to improve her English. She enjoyed his company but that was all. He was crestfallen. He had fallen in love for the first time in his life and she had used him, no, betrayed him.

Barclay sat on a bench on Gilmore Hill looking over the Kelvingrove Art Gallery and Kelvin Hall. This was the first time he had been in the precincts of Glasgow University since graduating. In his just ended fifth year at the College, Barclay had secured a permanent contract and had been interviewed for the post of assistant head of the department. He awaited the decision. It was a warm August day and he recalled the times when Mayne and he had lunch on what he was sure the same bench. He had received one letter from Mayne now in the army though not disclosing what he was doing or where he was.

He was aware of two girls on the bench to his left. They were laughing, and their accents disclosed they were Irish. Now, the two girls were off the bench and walking in his direction but behind him.

'Ian… Ian Barclay?' He turned his head back towards her. 'It's Bernie. Bernadette. Did English together.'

'Yes, of course.' He stood up and held out his right hand which was brushed aside in favour of a hug.

'This is my sister, Majella.' A handshake and they sat down on the bench with the man bracketed between the two girls. Majella was coming to study law at Glasgow in the coming session. Accompanied by their parents, they had been visiting the Yooni, arranging accommodation for Majella and staying on to attend an aunt's silver wedding party. The aunt and uncle had recently moved to Glasgow to escape the Troubles. So while their parents were doing last-minute shopping in Glasgow, the two sisters decided to have a stroll round the university. Barclay did not tell Bernie that this was his first return to the university since his graduation.

She changed the subject, 'How's that galoot Peter Mayne?'

'I don't know. He stopped teaching.' He decided not to mention the army. 'I don't know what he's doing or where he is.' Which was true.

He told her that he was still teaching in the same college in which Mayne's sister had secured them posts. He enjoyed it.

Bernie was teaching in a convent school in Magherafelt, her home town. She explained that when she was young they had to move to Derry when her father, a doctor, obtained a post in the hospital. Now they were back in Magherafelt because now he was working in the local hospital.

'Imagine having your sister as a teacher in the same school,' Majella interjected sourly. 'But she only got the wee ones, so I never had her.'

He did not want to mention the Troubles but asked if it was peaceful there because he had never heard of Magherafelt. 'The only trouble is caused by eejits from the townlands.'

'Townlands?'

'Small geographical divisions of land around the towns.' A concise answer indicating that Bernie had been asked the same question before and had framed an answer.

'Don't forget the Orangemen and their stupid flute bands. Some have even come from over here.'

'She's right but we try to ignore them. Otherwise it's fairly peaceful and the town is quite mixed.'

'Got good pubs.' Another interjection from Majella.

'You better not have been in any, young lady. If Mammy found out you won't be coming here' Her usual mischievous smile. 'But she's right. Some good pubs especially Mary's.'

'Mary's?'

'She owns and runs it…'

'Don't forget Phyllis,' said Majella. To Barclay, 'That's Mary's sister who helps her run it. Never any trouble in it. A mixed crowd – bankers and lawyers… and the teachers.'

No, he had never been to Ireland in response to Majella's question. He should visit. 'Bernie would look after you.'

'That's enough, Majella.'

'Could introduce him to the hairdresser. '

'No more, young lady. Anyway, we need to go.' The goodbyes were brief accompanied by mumbles of meeting again. When Bernie was about ten yards away, she turned back to Barclay, calling out, 'Your old girlfriend is making a name for herself. She's a lecturer at Queen's – in Belfast.' He feigned ignorance but it did not deter Bernie. 'She's active in the Troops Out movement or something like that. There's a lawyer we know who went to listen to her when he was at Queen's. Still the same old Christine, wanting to look after the downtrodden taigs.'

'I didn't know. Try not to take an interest in these things.'

'Your problem, Ian, was that you fancied the wrong Irish girl.'

In the same summer holiday, he attended his sister's wedding in Glasgow. It was a civil ceremony and thereafter a small reception in a near-by hotel. Her husband Niall Tait was an aircraft engineer employed by a small, Scottish airline. He was pleased to see his Aunt Hilda again who was alert and sharp but regretting having moved into the care home, and insisted it was his mother who needed to be in a home. Otherwise Glasgow did not hold any attractions for him.

In September, he was relieved to be back in London, and teaching. On his return the principal called him into his office. After the usual pleasantries, he handed Barclay a copy of the TES folded at an inside page with an advert circled. It was a teacher of English post at Sherborne School in Dorset. The principal explained that he was not trying to get rid of him but thinking of his future. It was time for him to progress his career. Normally, the masters at Sherborne were Oxbridge graduates but he knew Sherborne's headmaster. It did not mean that he would get the job but the headmaster would consider references from an old friend with long standing experience in teaching, in particular being able to identify good masters. He would assist him in drafting his letter of application. The principal was confident that Barclay would be given an interview, thereafter it was up to him. The principal's last piece of advice to Barclay was that he must not be so diffident as at his interview for his present post. He needed to be confident and purposeful but not arrogant.

Often, Barclay wondered why the principal was so supportive of him.

Thomas Yates, born and raised in Peterborough, had won a scholarship to Cambridge, reading Mathematics. Initially he found Cambridge unwelcoming and he was treated as an alien. He was at Cambridge when war came in 1939. Unlike many other students, he continued his studies being told that people with a degree in mathematics would be invaluable to the war effort. On graduating, he was insistent on joining the RAF and became a navigator in Bomber Command. Taking part in bombing raids over German cities led to simmering disillusionment with the morality of the strategy of the indiscriminate bombing of German cities. His simple but strong Christian faith caused anguish: his conscience wracked by guilt. A few of his comrades shared his views, others seemed to relish inflicting the death and destruction though the vast majority of aircrew adopted a cold, professional attitude that it was a job that had to be done. The fire-bombing of Hamburg in July 1943 had convinced him that he could not continue to participate in what he considered war crimes. Believing himself to be more culpable because it was his skills which took the aircraft to the target, he would refuse to take part in any further raids. And he was prepared to accept the consequences of his actions which would certainly not be as horrendous as for those poor souls at the end of the bombs. After confiding in his crew's skipper who was understanding, he did agree to one final mission which would be his skipper's last before promotion. He agreed not because of duty to uniform, king and country but out of an intense personal loyalty to his friend and comrade. Their Lancaster was damaged by flak over Germany then attacked by a German fighter. The skipper though wounded managed to land the damaged aircraft at Scampton in Lincolnshire. All except one of the crew had been wounded including Yates who had sustained serious injuries to his legs.

In the hospital, Yates and his skipper had both been told it was almost certain they would never be passed fit for flying. At the skipper's prompting, both agreed that neither would ever tell anyone of the navigator's intention to stop flying and the reason why. The skipper was posted to a training unit whilst Yates due to his mathematical skills was sent to a code-breaking unit. On their final meeting, they exchanged salutes, shook hands and muttered some pleasantries about meeting up. Yates thought he had glimpsed regret in his comrade's eyes. Yates never saw his skipper again. He mused that it was his punishment for his potential act of betrayal.

After the war, he took up teaching first in Peterborough then Bedford and finally as the principal in the college in Kensington. Approached by fellow Cambridge graduates to take up posts in public schools he declined. He made a number of trips to Germany, including to Dortmund, Köln and Hamburg, to atone for his sins. He was determined that in his own, small way he would do as much as he could to prevent or end conflict. His intention to take holy orders was pre-empted by meeting and marrying a wonderful Welsh girl.

As principal he felt some regret that he had not taken up the opportunity of teaching in a public school. He had allowed himself to be locked into his comfort zone. The young self-effacing Scotsman had reminded him of his own youth and his sense of dislocation when he first went up to Cambridge. Simply, he empathised with Barclay and wanted him to achieve as much as his knowledge and love of literature deserved. Yates had never had much interest in literature but like Barclay had a deep and enduring passion for his own subject and that was why he continued to take classes though there was no requirement for him to do so. Yates knew that the likes of Peter Mayne would always be successful because of the advantages provided by their backgrounds and therefore was determined to foster Barclay in order for him to have a successful career.

The interview at Sherborne was offered, and Barclay felt that it had gone reasonably well. He was told that he had performed admirably in the interview but there had been other out-standing candidates and that he would be informed of the outcome though there was the possibility that there might be second interviews. A few days later as he was leaving the school, the secretary asked if he would go to see the principal in his office. The principal told him that Sherborne had been impressed by him and that it was likely he would be invited to another interview. The principal understood that it was now a straight contest between him and one other.

When he returned to Rochester Square, later than normal, there was a note pinned to his room door stating: 'A Mr Mayne telephoned. He said that he would telephone you at about 8 pm.' Barclay could not read the squiggled name probably one of the postgraduate students.

Barclay was excited: Peter had not forgotten him. He had a mug of tea and a sandwich but could not eat. He wondered if Peter was close-by, no because he would have come to the house. At 7.30 pm, Barclay positioned himself by the downstairs pay-phone, guarding it to prevent another student from using it. He would tell any prospective users that he was expecting an urgent, personal call. Which was true. He snapped the receiver off at the first ring at the same time trying to keep calm.

'Hello. Ian Barclay speaking.'

'Ian Barclay?' The voice sounded the same as Mayne's possibly a tinge deeper

'Yes.' Expecting some Peter quip.

'Good. I am John Mayne, Peter's brother.' Barclay was concerned: Peter was alright or…? 'Peter probably told you that I might be in contact about a possible job.' A slight chuckle. 'Well the time has arrived. I don't have much time. Could you meet a colleague of mine for lunch about 1 pm on Friday – the day after tomorrow. Available?'

'I'm teaching.'

'Try to get some time off… or call in sick. It will be at the Saint Ermin's hotel in Westminster. Do you know it?'

'Yes.' His voice flat. He had been at a marriage in Caxton Hall with Veronica Amato and they had called into the hotel for a drink. Veronica was related to one of the waiters.

'Good. I will telephone about the same time tomorrow night to confirm your availability. Good man. Need to rush.'

The next night's telephone call confirmed the arrangements, and Barclay was to ask for Mr Ormsby's table in the restaurant.

It was not a problem for Barclay to attend the appointment. It was the first Friday of the month and the college had Mass at 1pm followed by a late lunch at 2pm. Provided he was back for his final class at 3pm, it was not a problem. The principal did not ask but presumed it was an interview for a teaching position, nevertheless, reminding him of Sherborne and not to be hasty in accepting any position if it was not a step up.

Godden was concerned, worried by the meeting in Londonderry with the brigade staff intelligence office, also attended by an infantry major who was coming to the end of a tour. He recognised the major. When Godden had been a colonial Special Branch officer, the major had been the sergeant of Colonel Gordon Buchanan-Henderson's covert troop. There were brief reminiscences. Neither man since their time in Shala had encountered the singular soldier who had returned to Singapore then left the army. They both agreed that the colonel, known as GBH, was excellent but atypical. The staff intelligence major had heard of the legendary GBH. The three agreed conducting intelligence operations had been easier in the colonies. Godden noted that both majors wore the wings of the SAS. Obviously, a mafia or akin to the masons within the army. He was wise not to express this opinion because the reaction from the two officers would have been direct and stinging.

Despite his serious concern, his attention was on the young lady sitting four rows in front of him on the early morning flight from Belfast to London. It could be a difficult meeting because she could be both brittle and uncompromising simultaneously. He did not wholly trust her though that was the nature of his business. He would be surprised if people wholly trusted him. A superior smirk.

She had told the organisers of the meeting not to meet

her at Heathrow because she was likely to be met by Special Branch officers and detained for hours possibly at a police station in London. Any welcoming committee was likely to be stopped also. She would make her own way to Islington. She had spoken at meetings in London before. She was right. Detained ostensibly by Special Branch officers and taken to one room then another where there was a change of clothing as well as the services of a make-up artist. The transformation into a dowdy, middle-aged professional did not take long. She picked up the leather, expensive briefcase. Her own clothes were stuffed into her cheap cabin holdall which would be returned to her later. No attention would be paid to this lady, a business woman, civil servant or possibly an academic.

She was shadowed by a security and counter-surveillance team to Paddington Station. She strolled to Marylebone Station stopping en-route for a coffee and sandwich engrossed in *The Daily Telegraph* which she abhorred: a leopard could not change all its spots. At Marylebone Station, she took a taxi to the St Ermin's Hotel. Godden was waiting for her in the lobby. A brief professional handshake and enquires about journeys: not their first meeting to any onlooker but not a close relationship. He told her that he was having lunch with a young man, a job interview. She declined the offer to join them, wanting to write her notes in preparation for the debrief, and would get something from room service. Godden told her that he should be finished by two and would come straight up. He knew the room number which was one of several rooms they retained in the hotel. His colleague John Mayne and he both thought it was time to use different places rather than this hotel with its long links to the intelligence community. It was about the only thing on which the two officers were agreed.

The lady paused watching Godden walk to the table. The

young man stood up and they shook hands. Barclay seemed surprised slightly confused. She was glad that she had declined the lunch offer. Godden could not be serious if he was trying to recruit Ian Barclay, her one-time fellow student at Glasgow University but Christine Latham would not mention it, indeed, she found it rather amusing.

His confusion was because Barclay had expected a Mr Ormsby. Godden explained they were colleagues but it was likely he would meet Mr Ormsby in the future. 'I am from a civil service department, well more a small analysis and research section.'

'I understand that Peter Mayne might have mentioned us?'

'Peter? Does he work for you?' A shake of the head by Godden. 'Yes. He did say something about… but that was years ago. I forgot.'

'Yes, but sometimes it takes time to identify the right post for someone.'

Barclay would not have a drink because he was teaching at 3 pm. Godden had a small red wine. They chose from the table d'hôte menu. Barclay was told to enjoy his lunch and then they would talk business. Godden was sure that he had not been as callow and nervous when he first sat in the same hotel about seventeen years ago. He could not recall the exact year. Past and unimportant information had been flushed from his mind in order to accommodate new and in some cases, alarming information. That was for another day.

Godden asked Barclay about university and teaching, without having any interest in the answers but alert to any words or phrases which might infer unreliability or a human flaw. Next, the intelligence officer asked him what were his favourite pieces of literature confessing that he had not enjoyed Shakespeare or poetry at school. Barclay replied, 'Difficult…

almost impossible to answer. There are so many.' He launched into a passionate discourse beginning with *Journey of the Magi*. Godden appeared interested, listening intently: a technique he had acquired over the years when sitting with someone usually a colleague though in reality often he was eavesdropping on or watching a target.

On this occasion, he was reflecting on the first time he had been in the hotel and the first time he had tasted a club sandwich. He was not treated to lunch in the restaurant but a bar lunch with a fellow old boy from Belhaven, a minor public school. He had dismissed quickly his then initial thought that it was a homosexual tryst. Ormsby had been direct and frank. It was the start of his journey beginning with being a colonial police Special Branch officer. What was the term Ormsby used? An 'unofficial'. He had joined formally the Secret Intelligence Service when he returned to England from his stint in South East Asia. His thoughts turned to his next meeting with his female agent. It was sheer luck she had come his way – right place at right time. Often the case in recruitment. He realised that Barclay had stopped. 'Very interesting. Think time to discuss matters.' He called the waiter over to clear the plates so there would be no interruption, and no, they did not want coffee without consulting Barclay. 'You have almost a photographic memory. I understand.'

Barclay was perplexed. 'No.'

'I was led to believe that you can remember long extracts from books and plays after reading them. Almost immediately.'

He shook his head. 'No. That's not true... well I can remember parts of books and poems but that is only after reading them a number of times. And yes, they do stay in my mind.'

Godden turned his head slightly to his left and in an aside

as if to a third party said, 'Peter shares the same trait as his brother – saying more than his prayers.' Barclay smiled not having heard Bernie's expression for some time. Godden had appropriated it from a school contemporary. If he did not have a photographic memory then he could not be used in the way Godden had planned. But he might be useful as an instant checking system if he did retain information once learned. Barclay was a clean skin and could be kept in the dark on the section's real role. When asked about Ulster, Barclay stated that he knew of The Troubles but he avoided discussion because it caused animosity sometimes among staff members.

Godden explained the Civil Service was setting up a new section to analyse the effectiveness of the police and army counter-terrorist tactics. The older man told him that coping with terrorism and internal security problems was one thing in the colonies when dealing with the natives but needed a different approach when happening on the streets of the UK. The new section would consider statistics, trends, weaknesses and subsequently make suggestions on how to be more effective. It was not being announced because once people know they are being monitored they act accordingly. ' You will of course have to apply to join the civil service and take the necessary examinations. However, because of the urgency, we would employ you on an *ad hoc* basis while you are completing the forms and process which is all quite boring. We will keep you away from other civil servants. They ask too many questions. There will be others employed on the same basis as you. What do you think?'

Barclay seemed uncertain. 'Sounds interesting, really interesting. But I'm not sure if…'

'Don't know unless you give it a go.' Godden paused and then smiled. 'It will just be like analysing a play except it's a modern one.'

Barclay smiled. 'I suppose so.' A morsel of enthusiasm in his voice.

'And you won't know the ending!'

Increased enthusiasm rendered with a broad smile. 'Yes, yes. I like that.' Though he remained unsure.

'Of course, civil service pay isn't great but with expenses… and likely accommodation to be thrown in, should be the same as your current pay possibly even higher. But we can sort that out later.'

'I see.'

'However, we will need to do a few background checks on you.' He saw the disappointment on Barclay's face. 'Don't worry. We all have to do them. Police checks that you have no convictions or any secrets.' A chuckle. ' You are not a Russian spy!'

Barclay smiled, 'Right, right. I understand.' He was thinking of his father. Would he have to explain the money from his father?

'We are hoping if the checks don't produce any problems, of you starting on the first of September. Means you can finish this term and have a holiday.' He took out a card then paused before staring hard at Barclay. 'It is very important that you do not tell anyone, and I mean anyone of this conversation.' He handed him the card. 'Think about it. Once you have decided, please telephone this number but speak only to me. Don't leave your name. If the background checks identify a problem we know how to contact you.'

The following weekend Barclay was having coffee with his sister in a cafe near Victoria train station. Her husband had obtained a job at Gatwick Airport with more money and better prospects than in Glasgow Airport. Her husband was house hunting around Gatwick. She was reluctant to leave her mother but could not turn down this opportunity. They were returning to Glasgow on the Sunday sleeper and moving down at the end of July. She was also expecting their first child. Perfunctory congratulations from her brother.

'Have you thought of returning to Glasgow?'

'No. Why should I?'

'Might be good to spend some time with Mum. She's fine, well okay.'

'You want me to nurse her?'

'No, Ian. I'm not saying that.'

'Could go into the home with Aunt Hilda.'

'Ian. She doesn't need to go into a home. But she misses you... and I thought you might want to see her more often.'

'I have a job down here – possibly might be getting another one, a better one, with more money. You don't have to leave Glasgow.'

'I told you. The job at Gatwick has more pay and better opportunities. You would get a teaching job in Glasgow easily.'

'I like my job here.'

'Fine, Ian. Let's not argue.' She changed the subject. 'Have you seen Dad?'

'No. Why?'

'He's not too good. He would love to see you again.'

'Don't want to. Still can't forgive him for what he did to Mum.'

She thought but did not say, 'You selfish little prick!' She decided not to tell him that their father's money would stop soon.

He finished his coffee and asked, 'He's not well?' Elaine

nodded. 'Is he still working?'

'Yes for the moment but he is planning to stop in the next few months.'

'Does that mean he won't be able…'

'Of course. You must have realised the money would stop sometime.' She could see her brother calculating and deliberating. 'I better go. Niall is waiting for me' She glanced at her watch and stood up. 'I don't want to miss the train.'

'Okay.' He didn't look up.

'Are you coming up to Glasgow during the holidays?'

'Maybe.'

'Better go. Bye, Ian. I'll give your love to Mum.'

'Right. Bye.' A tinge of a glance up.

He had hoped to buy a property in London but with his father's money drying up, it was unlikely he could afford anywhere suitable. He had telephoned Elaine when she was back in Glasgow. He was generous in his praise for her in caring for their mum but now it was right that he assumed the obligation. Family came first. He had been buying the *Glasgow Herald* in London looking at house prices. He asked Elaine to look for flats in Hyndland and other parts of the West End. During the call, she had smiled knowing their father's money or the soon lack of it was pivotal in her brother's decision-making.

Barclay acted quickly.

The principal had called him in. It was confirmed that he was being invited to a second interview at Sherborne. Barclay was so apologetic. He could not attend for the interview and was handing in his notice. His mother was ill and he had to return to Glasgow to care for her. His sister now pregnant was simply not able to look after their mother. The principal was sympathetic and understanding. Barclay was sorry to leave him in the lurch at such short notice. Barclay was not to worry. There were more and more English teachers becoming available. Anyway as the principal, he had to plan for the future and, anticipating losing Barclay, had identified two potential replacements though neither of his quality. Barclay was irked.

The principal repeated that he was not to worry mistaking Barclay's pique as guilt. Family came first and he was sure Barclay would obtain a post in Scotland. He could rely on an excellent reference from him. It would include the invitation to Sherborne's second interview. Barclay rather suspected no one had ever heard of Sherborne in Glasgow.

Barclay was not too disappointed in leaving London despite his claims to the contrary. He had fallen out of love with London. It was not exactly Paris or Vienna. The city had become dirty and inhospitable with too many grasping foreigners demanding their rights and privileges. Despite voting Labour, he considered Wilson followed by Callaghan as both incompetent and derelict in governing the country. Also, he had become bored of the anti-Scottish jokes which initially he had not minded finding them amusing, an example of English benign tolerance.

Godden had been the final straw, an arrogant, upper-class, English public schoolboy who had been smug and treated him with contempt. He had been dismissive when Barclay telephoned to inform him that he could not take the job because he had to return to Glasgow to care for his elderly mother. 'Unfortunate,' Godden had said. 'Think you might have been

rather good at it. However, these things happen. Goodbye.'
No thanks or offer to return if his circumstances changed. It
was cold indifference.

School Teacher: Glasgow

He had written to the Strathclyde Council Education Department which provided him with information on how to apply for jobs. Immediately after finishing the summer term, he returned to Glasgow for a week, reluctantly staying with his mother. There were a number of posts available but also a number of obstacles to be overcome. He secured a post teaching English in a Roman Catholic school in the north of Glasgow. The head of department or rather the Principal of English had been at university with him, and had benefitted from Barclay's assistance in writing essays. On seeing the circulated list of those seeking English posts, Stephen Lavery had telephoned Barclay's mother's home. The interview with the head teacher had not gone too well. There were questions about how he could contribute in extra-curricular activities which baffled Barclay. Nevertheless, Stephen Lavery was adamant that Barclay would be a good choice and more importantly would drive up the school's external examination results. The glowing report from the college had been significant especially when Thomas Yates had written that Ian had been offered a post at Sherborne School, usually reserved for Oxbridge graduates.

Barclay had been able to buy a two-bedroom flat in Hyndland rather quickly. The owners in the midst of a divorce were looking for a quick sale. Paying a large deposit and the small mortgage being well within his salary, he had converted into reality the aspiration which he first cherished when leaving Peter Mayne's Hyndland flat so many years ago. The only problem was that his mother refused to move in with him preferring to remain in her own home in Reidvale Street. She did visit him sometimes but he was expected to trail out to the East End even though there was a regular train service from Hyndland to Bellgrove train station which was just round the corner from his mother's home. Further, she appeared reasonably fit and healthy and not as his sister had described. He felt he had been misled.

Barclay was given only classes in the upper school, and also the top sets mainly due to Lavery being fed up with the demands of parents and the burden of marking. The principal was disillusioned: one time remarking to Barclay that teaching was the most difficult job in the world. Others, he continued, say that it is being a brain surgeon. 'No. Do you know why?' A shake of the head from Barclay. 'The brain surgeon's patient is unconscious when he has to face them. Our darling, little children sadly are not – though some are.'

It was the first time that Barclay had to teach girls, finding some of them quite challenging in their refusal to accept his interpretation of Shakespeare and other works. However, it was a mere irritant. He produced excellent exam results. The parents were mostly supportive and appreciative. Some of the teachers were put out that he was given all the top sets but not too outspoken. As in his previous post, he seldom went into the staff room preferring to remain in class offering support to the pupils.

He found most of the female members of staff pleasant and delightful: the male members were boorish with the only topics of conversation being football and politics, in particular the events in Ireland. A colleague in his department warned him to be wary in that some of the long-serving male teachers would prefer if he was replaced with one of their own, a football and politics man, and that these senior teachers exerted a great deal of influence on the recently appointed head teacher. Barclay discussed the matter with Lavery who confirmed it was true but told him not to worry because they, a disgruntled cabal, would not move while he remained principal.

In the December of his second year, Barclay's protective principal went off sick. It was diagnosed that he had picked up an infection whilst on holiday in Mallorca, and despite his determination, was unable to return being forced to take early retirement.

Lavery's successor adopted a different approach to her predecessor, believing all the teachers should share the same burden from first year to the top classes. Barclay found himself teaching first and second year classes as well as a third year class which consisted of disruptive and aggressive girls, and sullen and unmotivated boys. Most of the girls were insolent, lacking any respect for their teacher.

At in-service days, the head teacher and other senior management figures talked of empathy, understanding the individual pupil's environment and the deprived homes that many allegedly came from. Barclay could not see any evidence to support this claim, certainly not compared to his home environment when he was a pupil. His first warning or 'wee chat' with the new principal was a result of his refusal to allow the girls to go to the toilet during class. 'An excuse.' Barclay was reminded of the changes that girls go through, their periods, so they needed to be allowed to go to the toilet. He did have some allies from both male and female teachers, the latter usually the spinster type.

However, for most of his colleagues, it was wiser to remain silent and not challenge the new orthodoxies ruling the school. A history teacher compared it to Cromwellian rule; the new teachers and most in promoted posts forming the 'new model army' whilst musing it was rather an inappropriate comparison for a Roman Catholic School with many of the pupils being descendants of poor Roman Catholic Irish immigrants whose ancestors had suffered at the hands of Cromwell's rule. The history teacher's attitude reminded Barclay of his own fourth year history teacher who had been 'put to the sword'. Barclay asked his colleague who had warned him previously of other teachers whether the history teacher was safe in his job. His colleague laughed and said that the sardonic history teacher was very secure because his family had influence within the Catholic hierarchy, and probably more crucially, connections to Celtic Football Club. Barclay was astonished and appalled. The only outspoken rebel was the principal of the P E Department who at each staff meeting accused the senior management of appeasement of the pupils. He had little brains as opposed to his muscles twittered the puritan intelligentsia on the staff.

Barclay was dismayed by the use of four-letter words by the pupils including many girls. There had been swearing when he was at school but not to such an extent. He realised that he should not have been surprised when on his odd forays into the staff room, he encountered the same language.

In another 'wee chat' this time with the deputy head teacher, he was told that education was not just concerned with exam results but to develop the whole human being and it was essential for a teacher to understand the child and his or her world. The deputy head did not seem to take this too seriously and spent another ten minutes chatting about London where he had worked for a year.

The third 'wee chat' once more with the principal was that the texts, *Journey's End* and *The Lay of the Last Minstrel,* were in the past and not relevant to the world of today's pupils. Barclay thought but regretted that he did not remind the principal that he had not been in the trenches or around during the Border Wars. There had been complaints about the appropriateness of the texts from parents but in a spirit of compromise the principal would permit Barclay to continue teaching the offending texts to the end of the current session.

Barclay was dispirited and lonely. He realised that his drinking was increasing. The female teachers he liked were married, and the younger ones bored him. Some of his departmental colleagues seemed to lack any appreciation even interest in literature which for Barclay was an essential prerequisite for a teacher of English.

In the session beginning in August 1980 he introduced his fourth year class to *A Man for All Seasons*, the story of Sir Thomas More's clash with Henry VIII. Barclay was surprised that the Catholic pupils had no knowledge of this Roman Catholic saint, a true Catholic hero. The well-connected history teacher expressed the opinion that Thomas More might not have been the flawless saint of Barclay's perception. More disappointing was that the pupils with a few exceptions had no interest in Thomas More the great, English, Roman Catholic martyr. For these Catholic pupils, their heroes tended to be footballers: their hero worship stoked by most of the male teachers.

He began to yearn once more for London and thought of writing to Principal Yates but felt it would reflect badly on him. His reticence would not permit him. In the Catholic sixth form college, he had felt so alive and important, so integral and engaged. He remembered those cerebral masters, their eccentricities and good fellowship. But it was in the past. When he shared his views with a pleasant maths teacher originally from Leeds, the latter's response was that London was not England. It was a magnet for bohemians, people on the make and odd people. Londoners treated everyone north of Watford as dim and backward.

His Aunt Hilda died.

He noticed at the crematorium, the tall, reddish-haired, older man whom he had seen several times with an attractive woman in the Rogano restaurant in Glasgow. Barclay did not have the chance to speak to this unidentified man as he was gone as soon as the service was finished. As his aunt had promised, the fascinating letter on the mantelpiece was bequeathed to him. With an impatient sense of anticipation he read:

Dear Mrs Munro

I have written to you as a brother officer to your husband, Iain. When I first joined the Battalion, your husband was the company sergeant major.

He took me under his wing. He taught me so much not just military skills but in how to treat the soldiers especially the junior ranks.

He was an outstanding professional soldier who in his gruff manner cared deeply for his soldiers, young men far from home and often frightened. He told me that officers come and go in a

Battalion but the soldiers are there for most of their service.

When I got upset or angry about things not going well, he would tell me to calm down and not get frustrated.

As you know he was commissioned and became our company second-in-command. He remained calm and wise.

On the day of his death, our second platoon had been pinned down by fire. My platoon was to their left. Iain, not the company commander, appeared in my platoon area. I told him that I would move my men to help 2nd Platoon. He was adamant. It was a platoon pinned down not a section so it was a company task and having seen the ground he would lead the other platoon in a flanking attack whilst I gave supporting fire. Iain was killed at the end of the action. It turned out that he was the last person killed in our company by the Japs.

Iain was the most steadfast and modest soldier I ever met. He maintained his humanity no matter the conditions. I hated the Japs but I never heard him once abusing the Japs.

I am so sorry for your loss.

My sincere sympathy.

Yours Aye,
Gordon Buchanan-Henderson

In November, the friendly deputy head teacher called Barclay into his office. The deputy head and Stephen Lavery were friends and the latter would send his regards to Barclay via the deputy. Lavery retained links with selected members of staff. On this occasion, Lavery was warning Barclay that the vultures were gathering. Some of them were so spiteful and malicious that they could and would make his life a misery. His former principal's advice was to seek another school and he knew of a non-denominational school in the same area looking for a teacher of English for the term after Christmas. He thought that Barclay should apply for the post. The deputy concurred and told Barclay that he would ensure the head teacher gave him a good reference.

The non-denominational school provided a renaissance for Barclay.

The pupils were smart and enthusiastic. The large English Department consisted mainly of older women. The department was in an old building detached from the main school building so they tended not to interact with other members of staff. There was an authoritative air of calmness and order within the department with the teachers regarding themselves he thought as *la crème de la crème*. One or two of his female colleagues could have played Jean Brodie. His new colleagues were dedicated, knowledgeable and enthusiastic for their subject. Indeed, Barclay felt intimidated by most of them. Their knowledge and breadth of literature surpassed his. He realised he had been coasting after the first few years of his teaching career, simply teaching the same texts. Consequently he had to expand his knowledge and acquire new texts to teach. He discovered and embraced the work of Guy de Maupassant. His knowledge of Scottish literature was limited. He read Scottish texts such as *The Cone-Gathers* by Robin Jenkins and James Hogg's *Confessions of a Justified Sinner*. Moreover, he fell in love with a married colleague, Mhairi Tain.

He seldom walked the 100 yards up to the main building and then usually only for in-service days. At one, he was amused when a history teacher again – history teachers must have been first in the queue when irony and laconicism were being issued – likened the English Department to nineteenth century Britain being in *Splendid Isolation* though this would end when the new annex was completed and the department would be re-integrated into the school. Barclay was not impressed by another male teacher who said the move would end the teaching of Dickens in Dickensian conditions by repressed Victorian spinsters. He regretted not challenging this insulting and inaccurate description of his inestimable colleagues.

The move came. It reminded him of his childhood when families were moving from the grime and density of the tenements to the new housing estates like Easterhouse. Then, there was excitement with most embracing the change in their lives. The new estates were in the country-side with fresh air, and the houses even had inside bathrooms and toilets. Only later would the soulless nature of the estates become apparent.

Barclay did not embrace this move. A sense of loss of stability and security pervaded him. His inestimable colleagues were not perturbed by the change. The move into the main building was calm and orderly. The words of his headmaster Mr Cope reverberated in his mind, 'Remember, Barclay. *Resilience!*'

The noise especially at change-over at the end of each period was like a full symphony orchestra playing but out of tune and the audience not clapping politely but yelling and stomping their feet. Pupils pushed passed him not apologising and sometimes he felt they barged into him deliberately. Thankfully he had his own classroom so he remained within his room till the surge of human flotsam had passed. Foolishly, he had not realised the size of the school population which he should have done considering the numbers in the English Department. But his life had always been lived in a cocoon.

More alarming and shocking was the re-appearance of the disruptive, aggressive girls and sullen, unmotivated boys of his previous school. Some he had taught in the old building. How could a pupil transform from a gentle, obedient child into a scowling, disobedient fiend? He surmised that it was due to the school being an industrialised factory churning out animated and loud products not well-balanced, educated young people.

Politics was alive and well even in this middle-class school. There were never-ending grumbles about pay and conditions accompanied by talk of working-to-rule and even strikes. Barclay considered such talk was not befitting a profession. He was badgered by a wide-eyed maths teacher on joining the union. Barclay had never thought of and never felt the need to join a union. He joined as an act of appeasement in order to secure peace and quiet. Appeasement failed. The badgering did not stop. Why did he not attend union meetings, sign petitions, go on the protest rallies?

He became fed up with the constant arguments about politics, in particular, the bile poured onto Mrs Thatcher and the Tories. He had little time for Thatcher or the Tories but recalled the party in Mayne's flat where all the politics students no matter their label engaged with each other and shared a common pedigree of good manners and respect.

He watched several editions of what was almost the mandatory *Question Time* on BBC and decided Neil Kinnock sounded like a Modern Studies teacher never pausing for breath, Roy Hattersley was a bore and Cecil Parkinson was oleaginous. Only Denis Healey and Ken Clarke impressed.

The arrival of a new headmaster and shortly after a new deputy headmaster brought more disruption to Barclay's life. The headmaster was a prophet of the new mantras in education: assessment being not just about passing and failing; performance indicators; differentiation in both overt and covert forms with the latter being social class, race, gender and teacher's expectations; knowledge which speaks to their conditions; the individual centred curriculum; group teaching and informality.

The deputy headmaster's sole mission was to organise school activities to foster the corporate identity and spirit of the school as well as to make money. There were school sweat shirts for sale, fun days, non-uniform days to raise money for charities. The history teacher of *Splendid Isolation* compared the deputy to a street-trader character from a popular television show. Barclay watched it and was amused by a certain similarity. He did not continue to watch the programme finding it tedious though he actually found the deputy likeable and approachable.

Barclay continued to struggle with the less able classes and the introduction of mixed ability classes caused him more problems and anguished nights. On a number of occasions, he could not face school and stayed in bed. At the end of some classes, he felt physically sick. Sometimes, again unlike him, he would have a drink on a school night but it was on a Friday night when he embarked on what became known as binge drinking to the Sunday afternoon. His previous scrupulous preparation was declining and his marking of essays became desultory, lacking his normal extensive guidance to pupils which was not a problem during this session because he did not have any of the top classes in Higher or O Grade. He reasoned rightly that most of the pupils would not read his notes and he knew the texts so well that preparation was no longer necessary.

One day after he and his colleague Mhairi Tain, the furtive love of his life, had attended a training day at another school, they went for a drink. Mhairi asked if he was alright. She thought he seemed to have lost his enthusiasm. She understood it must be difficult with so many women in the department apart from one other male who was married and treated his female colleagues lightly.

'I don't want to pry, Ian, but if I can help.'

He was too timid to say, 'Apart from wanting you so badly.' Instead. 'I just find it difficult… controlling the classes especially third and fourth years. I wish I could be like Bob. He has no problems.'

Mhairi smiled. 'Don't be fooled. He has problems like all of us. He just hides it. He knows that he will get out of the classroom by being promoted.'

'But you don't have problems. The pupils like you.' Unsaid, 'I love you.'

'We all have discipline problems but you need to remember that we have been in the school for a while. We are established. Parents, their big sisters or brothers know us so they know not to play up.'

'Parents are complaining about me all the time.' Mhairi knew that it was an exaggeration.

'Teaching children is a heavy responsibility – and is very difficult. Most people think that they can teach. There's lots of frustrated teachers out there. Instead of a field marshal's baton in their knapsack, they have a piece of chalk.' A mischievous smile radiated her face. 'Ten minutes with 3C would soon cure them.' She paused. 'And that's why teachers are paid less than car mechanics.'

'Are they?' Barclay had little knowledge of what others were paid.

'I think so. Mind you, some of our colleagues don't help our cause by their attitudes and being downright lazy. Ian, don't be afraid to ask for advice or help anytime.'

He did not respond.

The deputy headmaster wanted a chat with him. He grinned as he said, 'There are good, bad and indifferent teachers.' A fleeting pause. 'Then there is Ian Barclay.' It was met with a melancholy frown. A failed attempt to lighten the mood of the meeting. 'Sorry, just teasing.'

Thereafter, he adopted a business-like tone though still friendly not stern. There had been complaints from a few parents about Ian's teaching. One mother wanted her son removed from his class because her son was not progressing. She claimed that Mr Barclay was not explaining things properly and in fact was picking on her son. Barclay responded feebly that he had tried to help him but the pupil was intent on being the class clown. The boy was not as clever as his mother claimed. He added that some of the parents believed that their children were more intelligent than they really were. It was unfair on their children: their expectations were unrealistic. The deputy headmaster was sympathetic but schools were different from their days. It was not anymore just about teaching, filling young minds with mathematic equations and the beauty of poetry, but managing expectations, avoiding conflict with parents especially the middle-class professional ones. However, the class clown would not be moved from his class which disappointed Barclay.

Matters settled for a short-time.

The next interview was with the headmaster. There had been further complaints from parents. In a stentorian tone befitting the headmaster of a school in a leafy suburb, he told Barclay that a teacher is not just there to teach a subject but to know and understand the whole pupil. Barclay thought how am I to do that when I see a pupil at the most in fifth year about four hours a week and even less in first year, and in the company of thirty other pupils? Furthermore, the classroom teacher had to get through a set, detailed curriculum. Barclay thought that the headmaster did not seem to be aware that he spent most of his breaks and lunch in his classroom providing additional support to pupils. The headmaster did not know or understand this whole teacher.

To provide guidance and mentoring to him, the headmaster would drop into Barclay's class from time to time. This had become his practice, popping into classes to support his teachers. He dropped in twice on Barclay's fourth year class and on both occasions the classes were respectful but sullen.

The next interview was according to the headmaster to provide some guidance on teaching methodologies. He thought Barclay was pitching his teaching at too high a level especially when teaching Shakespeare which was difficult for pupils. Shakespeare was alien to their life experiences, their backgrounds and environment. Barclay wanted to point out that when he was at school he was doing this particular play in first year, not fourth. Shakespeare was about conflict, family, loyalty, love which were part of their lives. The language was different but the lessons remained the same. It all remained unsaid.

The headmaster would discuss the best way forward for Barclay with the principal teacher of English. He informed Barclay that he was due to interview for a guidance teacher and the favoured candidate was an English teacher which could mean a reduction in Barclay's timetable. The headmaster was confident that a solution would be found which would be in everyone's interests, especially the pupils. Barclay refrained from commenting that earlier the main concern was to avoid conflict with middle-class parents.

His unhappiness and feelings of inadequacy continued. His drinking on school nights increased becoming noticeable to colleagues. Other teachers were drinking but this, to Barclay, was ignored as well as their other misdemeanours. The focus was solely on Barclay's ability and professionalism.

He was isolated: the failures of others were ignored. His ineffectiveness as a teacher was the *cause célebre* of the school.

He thought his colleagues were whispering behind his back and the pupils knew the guillotine would drop soon. Mhairi Tain remained supportive and showed concern for his health and wellbeing. Eventually, through a friend of his sister, he obtained a job with an insurance company. He resigned his post as a teacher in the middle of June before the end of the current session. Despite his pleas to the contrary, his resignation became public knowledge. Even some of the horrible female pupils expressed regret at his leaving: they claimed that they liked him. There were expressions of regret from colleagues including the headmaster and encouragement to remain. Good teachers were hard to find.

Hollow words!

In the long-established Scottish company, he was employed as a clerk responsible for preparing quotations for endowment policies and other savings plans. The interview with Mr Naismith the manager, immaculately dressed in a dark pin-striped suit, had been brief. He was not interested in why he left teaching. 'Teachers! Bloody mean buggers! Never buy a round in the club.' He looked at Barclay. 'Do you play golf?'

'No, sir.'

'Good. Don't want any threats to my dominance of the branch competition!'

After a few more questions, Mr Naismith offered him the job which he accepted. His start date would be the first of August, and he would receive a confirmatory letter.

On Barclay's first day in his new job, he was taken to the manager's office on the fifth floor to be welcomed formally. Mr Naismith welcomed the new employee at the door, shook his hand, escorted him to the chair in front of the large desk and then he sat down on the other side of the desk.

'You don't play golf?'

'Eh… no, sir.' He had been caught off-guard which he thought was intentional.

Mr Naismith's eyes went to his desk before he looked up and snapped, 'Why do you not play golf?'

Barclay shook his head. ' Don't know, sir. Just never have.'

'You won't get on… Play any sports?'

'No, sir. Never been sporty.'

He chortled, 'You'll get on well with Payne. Are you a mason?' He saw Barclay's questioning expression. 'A Freemason?'

'No, sir.'

'In the Orange Order?'

'No, sir.'

'You definitely won't get on.' He saw the disappointment in the new employee's face. 'Don't worry, Ian. It doesn't matter too much these days. And certainly not to me. This company was built on prudence, honesty and integrity. We are not second-hand car salesmen… unlike some of our rivals.' There was a knock on the door. 'Come in.' He nodded to the tall man who stood at the unclosed door, and turned back to Barclay. 'This is Mister Payne, our branch secretary. He will explain the set-up and show you the ropes. You will not see much of me. If you are in my office it will be because I am sacking or promoting you.' A smile. 'Or you are taking over from me. Off you go.' When Barclay was beside the branch secretary, Mr Naismith said, 'Remember, Ian, honesty and integrity are all you need to get on in this company.'

The branch secretary spoke with a standard Home Counties flat accent. Barclay's enquiry of where he was from was met with a mumbled 'near London'. He took Barclay down to the open plan office on the ground floor. Mr Payne as branch secretary had his desk at the back of the office overseeing two columns of four desks. Barclay's desk was the first in the column to Mr Payne's left, and it was the first after the reception area. The rest of the ground floor was taken up with three small interview rooms for clients and mostly rows of floor to ceiling metal shelves stacked with files.

The branch secretary told Barclay that he had received the standard introduction from the manager but not to ignore what he had been told. He explained that though it was called the Glasgow branch there were in fact three separate branches each with their own manager. The branch secretary called the three branches; Life, Motor and Building respectively which was followed by a hint of a smile. Payne's role was to be responsible for the mail coming in and going out, control the paper flow and allocate duties. Any applications for holidays were to be submitted to him. He explained to Barclay his duties, introduced him to the other staff in the Life office and concluded by seating him at his desk.

It was a drop in salary but Barclay still had some savings. He was fortunate in that he had saved money from his father's ill-gotten gains thereby not having to worry about a 25-year mortgage. His mortgage would be paid off in the next few years and he would own his precious Hyndland flat.

He did not consider that he had entered a new profession merely a job. He applied himself, learning the new world of endowment insurance policies and the number of years depending on the insured's age which would bring high returns. Sometimes when potential new clients, designated 'drop-ins', attended at the office, Barclay met with them when a salesman was not available. The drop-ins were usually young professionals embarking on their careers. Most were impressed by Barclay's quiet, professional service never engaging in high-pressure sales techniques – he did not know any – to which they had been faced in other companies. He was awarded with bonuses which did rile some of the salesmen who complained to the manager. Mr Naismith did not budge, telling the salesmen that the company could not wait till they were available. Anyway, they spent too much time on the road, following up leads. Instead, he promoted Barclay to be a section leader supervising three other clerks doing the same job. Barclay speculated that Mr Naismith considered the salesmen as second-hand car salesmen. It was an easy job for the former teacher. And he realised that this was the first time he had been promoted.

Mr Payne the branch secretary was unpopular with most of the staff being described as 'fastidious', 'pedantic' and 'a pain in the arse'; nevertheless, Barclay found him helpful and patient though he would never engage in conversation on any subject except the minutiae of life insurance.

Barclay saw his mother at least once a week either visiting her or as he much preferred she coming to Hyndland. The death of her sister Hilda had affected her. His sister Elaine now had two children which stopped her visiting as often though Barclay thought it was an excuse. She had wanted her mother to come to England to live with her but their mother would not even consider it.

Elaine spoke to her brother on the telephone at least once a week encouraging him to see more of their mother and reiterating the effect on her of the loss of her sister Hilda. Barclay protested that he did see his mother and had wanted her to move into his flat. That's why he bought a two-bedroom flat. Elaine explained that their mother felt more comfortable and at ease in her own little home in the Reidvale area which she knew. Hyndland to their mother was like a foreign country. He scoffed at this suggestion but knew that his mother was uncomfortable coming to see him as everything was expensive to her. When he took her for tea or a meal, she would take only tea and a sandwich or cake. She did not want Ian wasting his money on her. She enquired about girlfriends, wishing he would settle down with a nice girl which he dismissed offhandedly so she learned not to mention it.

In the July before the end of his first year with the insurance firm, Elaine was in Glasgow for the two children to see their gran. She told Barclay that their father was very ill, in fact he was dying. She had told their mother who had stared blankly at the wall and said nothing. She had not mentioned the money that her husband had provided to her through Elaine.

Barclay would not entertain her suggestion, her plea to visit their father. 'Please, Ian. He is desperate to see you again.'

He shook his head. 'No. I still can't forgive him.'

'You are so stubborn. Not heard of forgiveness.'

'I am not a Catholic. Peter was always wracked with guilt and preaching the need for forgiveness.' An exaggeration. Elaine presumed he meant the tall, handsome English boy who had taken them for a meal after Ian's graduation.

'You're like one of those old, Wee Free ministers!' Her voice was raised in condemnation.

He thought of the minister in Iain Crichton Smith's *Consider the Lilies* but unlike the minister he was not betraying the old woman Mrs Scott, on the contrary he was being loyal to his mother. 'I know he treated Mum badly but he is still your father.' She looked round the well-furnished flat. 'You couldn't have afforded this without his money.'

'That was only him paying his dues. Reparation for the damage he did.'

Elaine shook her head in anger and picked up her handbag. She paused, looking down at him. 'I'll see myself out.' She opened the living room door, paused and looked back at him sitting in his chair. 'You really are a selfish wee prick!'

His father died five days later.

Circumstances changed with the old, established Scottish company being taken over by an international conglomerate. A young, enthusiastic manager, Mr Cameron, arrived. He was bursting with new ideas and management-speak, being a constant repetition of jargon which Barclay did not understand.

It was not enough to sell one policy to the young professionals but these customers had to be made aware of the whole range of the company's products, pension plans and other investment vehicles rather than the almost redundant endowment policies. Barclay was uncomfortable with this new approach. The customers should be offered only what they needed instead of subjecting them to hard–sell techniques to entice them to purchase products which they could not afford. Such conduct breached the values of honesty and integrity of the old company.

The work had become boring and inconsequential which Barclay alleviated by delving further into literature.

After Cameron's friendly chat with Barclay which included the words of caution in regard to heavy drinking, his relationship with the manager continued to deteriorate. There were further verbal warnings. He deduced that Cameron's conduct in the same way as the head teachers of the two Glasgow schools was intended to drive him out.

Barclay received the letter through the internal mail system. It was just before 5 pm. He read it quickly. As anticipated it was a warning as to his future conduct. References were made to inefficiencies, not giving proper respect to his colleagues and concerns that his use of alcohol might be impacting on his work. He re-enveloped the letter, stuffed it into his right-hand jacket pocket and stood up. He was aware of another clerk, Bob Jardine, observing him, no doubt aware of the letter's contents. He always seemed to know the office gossip and what was coming from the fifth floor. It was rumoured that Jardine was in a relationship with Mr Cameron's secretary though both were married. As he passed Jardine's desk, he said, 'Good night.'

'You should get a lawyer.' In a low almost conspiratorial voice.

Barclay said, 'I'll speak to Mr Cameron in the morning.'

Jardine watched him go to the door before muttering, 'And pigs will fly.'

Major Charlie Scott was seated. He exuded an air of authority, effortless as well as patronising with a tinge of exasperation like a gentleman's gentleman having once more pointed out the errors of his ways to his young gentleman. A Jeeves, yes, exactly. Barclay had read a couple of P G Wodehouse's books on train journeys. The first one was slightly amusing but he became bored by the retelling of the same story. But, of course, Dennis Price had played Jeeves in the television series *The World of Wooster*. Barclay had watched it at the behest of Peter Mayne who had laughed at situations in which Barclay failed to find anything remotely funny or even amusing. Dennis Price played Charlie Scott in the film of James Kennaway's *Tunes of Glory*.

Acting Lieutenant-Colonel Jock Sinclair, DSO (and bar) was right when he had told Scott, '… *you've a mind of your own…*' The charge Scott had to answer was whether he had used that *mind of his own* to undermine, no, to betray his wartime comrade.

'You were jealous of Jock Sinclair?'

A look of disdain from the witness.

'You betrayed him because Mary Titterington rejected you in favour of Jock?'

'*We can't have chaps poking corporals in the eye, after all.*'

Barclay knew it was wrong for a colonel to strike a corporal. ' You can forgive one minor indiscretion. It will finish Jock.'

'*That is a pity.*'

'Major Scott, it was Jock. You both had fought throughout the war in the desert… Italy, France… eh… Germany. You were comrades.' His tone became lower and beseeching, almost begging. 'Out of personal loyalty.'

'*We've got to think of the Battalion sometimes.*'

Barclay knew that it was futile to continue. Cairns had told him that simply repeating the question would not get a witness to change his answer and would in fact make the witness more confident and steadfast.

The next morning after Major Charlie Scott's interrogation more a mild, ineffectual cross-examination, Mr Cameron said in passing that redundancy might be the best option to resolve the situation. During the morning break, Bob Jardine sought out Barclay to tell him that Cameron could not make him redundant. It was illegal. Barclay should consult a lawyer, an employment lawyer. Barclay did not bother to ask Jardine how he knew.

Barclay considered asking Cairns to recommend an employment lawyer. No, he probably did not know any because he represented only criminals. And he preferred to keep his affairs private.

Identifying an employment solicitor from the Yellow Pages, an appointment was arranged for 5.15 pm. It was a five minute brisk or ten minute leisurely walk from his office in St Vincent Street to the solicitor's office in Union Street. The solicitor, Mr Dougan, asked a number of questions, some of which Barclay could not provide answers to because the redundancy procedure had not been initiated. Mr Dougan made notes but did not or as he said could not provide legal answers at this stage. He would write to Barclay confirming what was discussed and advising on the next course of action. The meeting had lasted thirty-five minutes.

The letter arrived just over two weeks later. It did confirm the information Barclay had provided but with no clear or practical legal advice offered, with 'depending on' being the relevant factor. A scale of fees was included for his information in the event that he wished to instruct their firm in this matter. A fee note for £112 plus VAT was enclosed, and that payment should be made within the next seven days. He paid the fee though he did not provide any further instructions to the solicitor.

The departmental meeting had been routine, an update on the targets met and those still outstanding which indicated the set yearly target would not be achieved. Mr Cameron did not want recriminations among the staff or for anyone to engage in the blame game. They were a team and he was confident that with some more effort, a bit more drive, the target could be achieved. He would send a memo to each section leader with suggestions on how to up their game, and he wanted a memo from each section leader with their suggestions. They should consult with their excellent boys and girls who were bound to have good and innovative ideas. Cameron declared that it might be time for another team-bonding exercise which always succeeded in motivating everyone. This was a reference to a Friday spent at a hotel with the staff being mixed into groups that competed in physical and mental exercises ending with a meal with all expenses being met by the company. The aim, no, the mission was to create an inclusive corporate identity.

At the end of the meeting as they were dispersing, Cameron liked to have a brief, private word with each section leader. He told Barclay that he expected the situation to be resolved very soon once Head Office had agreed his plan. Barclay ruminated on his choice of language not 'approved' but 'agreed' implying equality of power.

In the supermarket, Barclay had decided to buy some smoked haddock not because it was Friday but because it looked fresh. Although he knew few Roman Catholics who continued to observe the practice, he liked abstaining from meat on a Friday because he liked fish, and he deemed that it brought him closer to Sir Thomas More in character and spirit. He had baked the fish in the oven, and poached an egg. He was proud, no, not exact enough, pleased that he had always been able to cook even if only simple dishes. The secret was preparation and not to rush the cooking. It was a deliberate process like writing an essay.

One whisky after his two glasses of wine with the fish would be sufficient. He read the case-notes. He felt confident. Finally, Barclay had Thomas Cromwell in his sights. It was an unexpected appearance. Cromwell would have to account for his ruthless hounding of Sir Thomas More, a good and honourable man.

'You said yourself that… let me quote: "*Now our present Lord Chancellor – there's an innocent man.*" Why did you bring charges against an innocent man?'

'*It's much more a matter of convenience, administrative convenience.*' Thomas Cromwell was podgy. The actor Leo McKern who portrayed Cromwell in the film of Robert Bolt's *A Man for all Seasons* had been in the Beatles' movie *Help*, playing a high priest or something, and he vaguely recalled him in a war film set in Burma or somewhere. Fleetingly, It reminded him that his uncle Iain Munro had been killed in Burma. A corpulent Leo McKern did not seem an intimidating Cromwell but most certainly a devious one.

'It was not an *administrative convenience*! You brought him to trial on a charge of high treason!' He was shouting. That was wrong! He had to remain in control.

'*… there never was nor never could be so villainous a servant nor so traitorous a subject…*'

'You had no evidence!'

Silence.

'You used the evidence of a perjurer against him!'

Silence.

'So you admit that? You admit you used the evidence of a…' He said almost inaudibly, 'Silence gives consent.' He had lost the thread of his cross-examination. He couldn't be bothered consulting the file.

'*The oath was put to good and… faithful subjects… up and down… they declared His Grace's Title to be just and good. And when it came to the prisoner he refused.*' Donald Pleasance in his SS uniform sneered menacingly. Barclay was confused, nevertheless he would not be intimidated. Barclay rose unsteadily to his feet. 'You murdered a… good…' In his anger, he had knocked over the wine table causing the glass and the book of the play to fall to the floor. On his knees to pick up the two items, he began shouting and banging on the coffee table. He was aware of clattering into the furniture and the doors as he made his way to his bed.

The following morning, Miss Boyd owner of the flat directly above him, was waiting for him as he locked the inner door of his flat. 'Are you alright?' Barclay mumbled yes, feeling embarrassed and dishevelled, smelling of alcohol. 'I was concerned that you had an intruder. Even thought of telephoning the police.' It was an appeasing lie – Miss Boyd, a refined lady of indeterminate age would not tell any other type. She had manoeuvred him into the vestibule between the inner and outer doors. It was a limited but confidential space.

'You can't go on like this, Ian.'

They had had a drink together in the local pub on three occasions. The first time, he was having a drink when he noticed her with a male and a female, surmising they were colleagues. When they were leaving, she noticed Barclay sitting on his own, telling her colleagues that she would see them in the morning, she asked if she could join him. She liked to know who was living in her close. To make sure that he was not a maniac. She was teasing him. Morag Boyd worked for the Greater Glasgow Health Service. She was not a doctor, not a nurse, just in administration. She gave him a potted history of their neighbours though only disclosing sketchy details of her life. The fact that once Barclay had been a teacher did not surprise her. On the other two occasions, they had bumped into each other at the close entrance, with first Morag suggesting they go for a drink and on the second it was Barclay's suggestion. There was never any hint of a relationship developing, and Barclay thought she was avoiding him because they seldom bumped into each other. She did say that she travelled a lot for work which was confirmed by Mr Cairns, the lawyer.

In the vestibule, she told him frankly, 'You need to get help.' It was her concern for his welfare that stopped him from telling her not to interfere in his private life. Though he knew that was not true.

'I know but...'

She did not allow him the opportunity to manufacture an excuse. 'I know people. I could arrange something.'

'No, no. It's okay.'

'It's not.' She paused looking at him but his eyes were downwards. 'Promise me that you will at least go to see your GP.'

'I will.'

'Promise me, Ian.'

He felt like a little boy being asked to promise not to commit some misdemeanour again.

He did go to his GP who was nearing his retirement. He was sympathetic. He told Barclay that physically there was nothing wrong with him apart from drinking too much which was accompanied by an emphatic understanding look.

'If I am to help you, Mr Barclay. May I call you Ian?'

'Yes. Of course.'

'If I am to help you, Ian, you must be honest with me. Totally. Like being in the confessional.'

'I'm not a Roman Catholic, doctor.'

A wry smile. 'Be a Catholic Protestant... for a short time.'

Barclay thought Peter Mayne would have liked that, and probably would have wished that he had thought of the axiom. In fact, he recalled that Peter had initially thought him to have been a Catholic. Peter had declaimed, 'You're like a Catholic, always wracked with guilt – even over minor things such as not getting an essay in on time.'

'Where do I start?'

'From your childhood.' Barclay was surprised. Was his GP a frustrated psychiatrist? The patient started from his first day at secondary school sitting outside the headmaster's office when he thought that he would be turned away. The GP turned away from Barclay, picked up his pen and began making notes. He did not look at Barclay even when questioning him which was to expand on or clarify a point.

Barclay ended with the relationship with his manager who was trying to get rid of him. The latest proposal was to make him redundant. As when teaching, he sometimes felt nausea, headaches, tension, no, fear in the pit of his stomach, not wanting to go to work, anxious to avoid confrontation and unpleasantness. He admitted to lacking self-confidence and self-esteem, being unable to relate to others. Alcohol was the only cure for these symptoms, and it also enabled him to sleep. He was not optimistic about his future.

The GP finished making his notes, placed his pen carefully in its allocated place on the desk, reread some of the notes, looked up at the clock on the wall. 'My daughter will be telling me off. You have been in here for almost forty-five minutes' He turned to Barclay. 'She is replacing me. She is very keen, efficient. Full of new ideas. Does not want patients to be kept waiting. Twenty minutes at the most for a consultation. If we cannot make a diagnosis in that time, then the patient should be on his or her way to the hospital.' He laughed, more a guffaw. Barclay thought the daughter was a medical Cameron.

'I am going to refer you to a psychiatrist.' He held up the

open palm of his right hand. 'Don't give me any nonsense about it not being a manly thing. Need to be strong and not display any emotion. Piffle! More men could have been helped even saved by seeing a psychiatrist. In this I am more modern than my daughter.' Another wry smile. 'She can be quite hard. Men should man up. Be strong! Think she's a Thatcherite.' His gaze returned to the wall. 'She has never seen the effects of war.' He turned back to Barclay. 'In today's harsh and unforgiving economic climate – with the unemployment, many men no longer are the breadwinner. It affects them. Everything is about making money not the value of human life.' Once more looking at his patient he said, 'I'm sorry. Excuse my tirade.' Barclay did not respond. 'Will you go?'

'Yes.'

'Good. It will help you though it might take a few weeks for the appointment to come through.' Barclay gave an understanding nod. 'In the meantime, I am going to give you a sick line for fourteen days. I will mention you are being referred to other services but not name them.'

'Thank you, doctor'

'Ian, it will be better if you avoid alcohol at least for the next fourteen days. I know how difficult that can be, but try.'

'I will, doctor.' He stood up. 'Thank you very much for your help, doctor.'

A jovial 'don't mention it' wave of his right hand by the GP.

Barclay had not been totally honest by failing to disclose to his GP his own alcohol-fuelled interrogations in his sitting room. He had usually forgotten about them the next morning. He knew that he was not being totally honest with anyone even himself.

He did not drink during the next seven days. It was stressful. He fought the urge to drink by long walks, visits to the cinema and the library to peruse the newspapers. One day a brief headline on an inside page caught his attention: *Lecturer Murdered*. He read the article: *Christine Latham a lecturer in English at Queen's University was shot dead near to the University. Miss Latham though a Protestant had been active in opposing the British Army in Ulster. She had spoken at Sinn Fein meetings and at a number of Troops Out rallies and meetings in England. It is believed that Miss Latham was murdered by Loyalists though no group has claimed responsibility.* He picked up another paper, a tabloid, which contained the same story but in more lurid and sensational details. It inferred that the Protestant lecturer had got what she deserved for being disloyal to her own people and her country. Feeling sick, he left the library quickly to return home. Initially, he resisted the temptation to drink in order to ease the pain. Christine, his one true love, would not have wanted him to remember her through an alcoholic haze. He succumbed to the whisky. He did not venture out during the next three days due to feeling a sense of inconsolable loss, and a deep hangover.

Miss Boyd visited him and they went out for dinner. Mr Cairns had also taken him out to the local pub. Barclay contented himself with a soft drink, Irn-Bru. When he had first moved into his flat, he had been invited up to the lawyer's house for drinks a couple of times. Each evening followed same procedure, his wife would excuse herself because she had chores to do, thereafter Cairns talked about the law, well, his part in the application of justice in Glasgow Sheriff Court and sometimes beyond in Airdrie or similar towns. Unlike many of his fellow lawyers, he claimed that he did not mind going to trial. He had been a procurator fiscal before becoming a criminal defence lawyer. He had seen it from both sides, prosecution and defence. The technique of leading evidence or cross-examination was very different. Defending, he tried to avoid having his clients give evidence but if they did they should keep their answers short. Each time, it was the same monologue of his endless triumphs in court, his bettering of his opponents and tussles with the sheriffs, sometimes having to correct a sheriff on a point of law. His neighbour was steeped in overweening confidence. Moreover for Barclay, it was a crash course in criminal justice though he did harbour doubts over the credibility and reliability of the averred courtroom triumphs.

He did not reveal to his two neighbours his suffering from the tragic loss of Christine. He considered going to the funeral whenever and wherever it took place. The day before his return to work, he read that the private funeral had been in England. He did not understand why.

Barclay felt better but not enthusiastic on his return to work. His manager was welcoming but wary. It took only a few days for the manager's criticisms to begin, minor ones at first. In private, Cameron told the returning Barclay that he, Cameron, had personally undertaken a review of Barclay's paperwork which had revealed some discrepancies, mainly due to a lack of attention to detail. In this current economic climate, this can cause a loss to the company even major complaints from clients that could lead to legal action, again causing a financial loss to the company. Barclay asked the nature of these mistakes. Barclay thought of his teaching and the need to always highlight and explain the mistakes to a pupil so he or she did not repeat them. Moreover, Cameron told him that he *personally* had been responsible for rectifying the mistakes which he undertook in order to save Ian any embarrassment. The offending documents had been destroyed and replaced with new ones so unfortunately he could not show him the actual mistakes. That was unhelpful and bad practice but Barclay did not express these thoughts.

Also, it had come to Cameron's attention that when he was off sick, Barclay had been seen out in restaurants and pubs. He knew the sick note was not a confinement order but it suggested a lack of loyalty to his colleagues who had to cover his work. Barclay failed to remind Cameron that he had said that he *personally* had dealt with his work.

When he mentioned to the branch secretary – whom he now regarded as, if not an ally as at least a sympathetic neutral – the manager's comments on being in pubs and restaurants, Mr Payne said that it was an infringement of his private life. Further, he should record everything Cameron said to him, and inform him that he was doing it. Barclay could be certain that Cameron would be doing the same without informing him.

A staff meeting had been announced for 5 pm with close of business being at 5.15. Notwithstanding that it was a full staff meeting of all the different departments not just the Life office and he was not the most senior manager, Cameron made the announcement. There was going to be a world-wide restructuring of the company but beginning in the UK. The consequences of the restructuring would be a leaner, more efficient and more profitable company. He paused, smiling as if waiting for the applause. None came. Staffing levels would have to change due to the closure of some offices, and the centralisation of some activities into the Head Office. Glasgow would not be closing. Head Office recognised that we are now an efficient, lean, mean machine. Cameron paused to display his enthusiastic, self-congratulatory grin. Of course there would have to be some changes. Details would be announced in the next few weeks so it would probably be best to wait until then for questions. Staff could finish now for the day. A placatory carrot. Barclay heard someone behind him in a mock whisper say, 'He really does think that we are fools.' The three managers turned away.

'It means job losses!' Not a question but a recognition of reality from a claims handler in the motor insurance branch. He was known for his outspokenness and his attempts to unionise the work-force. The managers turned back to face their staff.

'You should know by now, Bill, that restructuring means jobs going.' It came from his manager, a gruff Geordie from Gateshead.

'So I'll be for the chop this time.' Again, not a question.

'I would think so.' Cameron's visible displeasure increased more following his fellow manager's next comment which was accompanied by a roguish smile. 'I'm likely to be on the chopping board with you.' This brought laughter.

Some of the staff as was their custom, more a tradition, on a Friday decided to repair to the pub round from the office. Bill was encouraging others to join them. Barclay thought he could not refuse the branch secretary's suggestion to join them. As far as he was aware the secretary never went to the pub with staff. He was management. Barclay felt the secretary and other colleagues had caged him so he could not escape on the short distance to the pub.

In the pub, after the first drinks, Bill was encouraged to make a speech, and not needing much encouragement made a short, witty speech on the need to organise and fight the job losses. This was met with some clapping by the younger members of staff but by good natured jeering from the longer serving employees who knew from experience that they would not win any fight. In other unionised industries despite the strikes, mass rallies and high-level meetings with government ministers, the job losses were not prevented. The Tory Government was on the side of big business: it was a symbiotic relationship.

The branch secretary and Barclay shared a bottle of red wine, chosen by and paid for by the former, his treat. 'I will be on the chopping board,' he said in his quiet, home counties accent. Barclay's expression was one of surprise. 'Yes. My job is out-dated to our thrusting, modern manager. I know it will disappear. It has already because Mister Cameron opens and signs all the mail. In fact, I am taking money under false pretences. When you were off, I covered your desk.'

'Cameron told me he had reviewed my work,' said a surprised Barclay, 'and he found a lot of mistakes.'

'There were some, Ian.'

'Cameron said he had destroyed some documents and replaced them with new ones.'

'Absolute nonsense!'

'Should I go to see an employment solicitor?' He did not tell him that he had consulted one previously but felt it was a waste of money.

'You would have to go through the internal grievance procedure first.'

'Oh.' Bob Jardine had not mentioned that.

'But, I would advise you to take any deal offered. I intend to.'

'Are you?'

The older man took a sip of wine. 'But, it's not a problem

at my age. My children are grown up and gone. There's just my wife who is a bit younger than me and still working – probably will work for a few more years. We have some savings and the mortgage is paid off. I was fortunate to take out endowments which produced excellent returns on maturity. Also, subsidised mortgages used to be on offer.'

'What are you going to do?'

'More time for my hobby. Horse-racing.'

'You bet on the horses?' A question from a surprised verging on stunned Barclay.

'A little. Watch it on television. But it's going to the races, watching and enjoying the atmosphere. The smell.' He smiled at Barclay's reaction. 'Studying the form is a science. There are a number of factors to consider before placing a bet. It's like preparing a quotation for a client. There are questions to be asked.' He paused, smiling at Barclay's reaction.

Apart from watching horse racing a few times on television, Barclay's only experience of people betting on horses was when he was young, watching the police raid the closes from where the bookies operated illegally. The police would take people away but within weeks the same people were back in business in the same closes or near-by.

The branch secretary continued. 'It's a good social life and we have made many friends. Thankfully none working in insurance. We hope to get to the Kentucky Derby one day.' He took another sip of wine. 'The secret is moderation in gambling... and this.' He held up his glass of wine. 'I have had enough and you will have to finish the bottle.' Barclay smiled in appreciation though still surprised at the revelations of this dull, soft-spoken, pedantic man. 'But, Ian, our grating-ly enthusiastic branch manager is right about alcohol being a career stopper.'

'But some of the other clerks drink. Why has it not stopped their careers?'

'It has. They are not going any further. Clerks in their late thirties, mid-forties. You know who I mean. They can do their job even if wrecked with alcohol. It's an easy job once you know the ropes. With the amount of drinking they do, they are almost immune to it. They can function at a low, un-complicated level with a high level of alcohol. They probably know how much they can drink each night which still allows them to work without making mistakes.'

'I understand.'

'Do you? You drink too much. And unlike your colleagues, alcohol controls you.'

Barclay looked down, stung by the frankness. 'It's Cameron. He's on at me all the time. Always finding fault… and as you know, he tells lies.'

'I know but that's why you should take any offer. You need to get out of this business. But you need to find a job which challenges you, keeps you busy – and off the drink.'

'You're right. But…'

'Why not go back to teaching?' Payne interjected.

He shook his head. 'I can't. Not here in Glasgow. Maybe in London.'

'Well, go to London!'

'I can't… my mum's here and I need to look after her.' His tone was sad almost self-pitying.

The branch secretary took a sip from his glass though it was empty. 'I have a neighbour. He took early retirement and went back to university to do a PhD. He's almost finished and is confident that he will get a teaching job at the university. Think it's Strathclyde. And he's older than you. He's in his late forties. I think. You should enquire about it.' He stood up.

'Thanks. I will.'

'See you on Monday. Goodnight.'

'Goodnight.'

The branch secretary took two steps away then half-turned towards Barclay. 'You need to keep yourself occupied!'

Barclay refused drinks from other colleagues. He picked up a curry on his way home. It was Friday. In the dining kitchen he had two cans of lager while eating the curry.

Now after the red wine and the lager, it was whisky on the table. Tonight, it was the Jean Brodie file on the table beside the crystal glass. The 'file' was his mature copy of Muriel Spark's *The Prime of Miss Jean Brodie*, her most famous novel but not in Barclay's view her best.

Sandy Stranger now Sister Helena of the Transfiguration or, confused, was it Sister Mary Joseph his colleague in London. It was Mary Joseph who sat on the sofa not in the witness chair. Why? Was she making a point? She should not be accused of a crime.

He stared at her, perused the file and began the questioning. He would prepare the ground to win her confidence. 'Do you remember any of your teachers from Marcia Blaine School?'

'*There was a Miss Jean Brodie in her prime.*'

'Why do you remember her?'

Silence.

'Was she a good teacher? Do you remember anything she said?' He realised his error in that you should ask only one question at a time. He had learned that in Cairns' crash legal course.

'*Give me a child at an impressionable age, and she is mine for life.*' That was a Jesuitical doctrine.

'Anything else?'

'*If only you small girls would listen to me I would make of you the crème de la crème* .'

'Anything else?'

'*One day, Sandy, you will go too far.*'

'What did she mean by that?'

No reply. No it was a stupid question because Sandy would not know. 'Did you say "*She was an Edinburgh Festival all on her own.*"?'

Silence. Confused. He would need to consult the file. Possibly it was another girl. He knew that his ability to recall the file notes without referring to them was fading. He flicked through the file but could not find the relevant part and he was finding it difficult to focus on the words. It was becoming hot. Another sip of liquid. The nun remained unperturbed. He was losing the thread of the cross-examination. He realised he had to come to the crux quickly.

' Joining the Roman Catholic Church was a deliberate act to antagonise Miss Brodie?'

Silence

'You told the headmistress that you were interested… eh… "*only in putting a stop to Miss Brodie.*" Why?'

'*She's a born Fascist…*'

He had to put the charge to her. 'Why did you betray Miss Brodie?' An accusing finger aimed at the nun.

'*It's only possible to betray where loyalty is due.*'

He could not continue. He needed the toilet.

The details of the restructuring as they affected Glasgow were published ten days after the initial announcement. The three branches were becoming one with Mr Cameron appointed as the manager. There would be the loss of a number of posts. Those employees affected would be called into the manager's office for a confidential interview. Barclay was the first interviewee. Cameron was friendly even effusive. This way would avoid any need to go down the route of compulsory redundancy. The company had an offer for him which he Cameron had insisted be increased.

Cameron had become alarmed when the branch secretary had raised with him the covering of Barclay's desk when he was off sick, and obliquely told Cameron he knew of his lies. He hinted at the possibility of legal action by Barclay because of the claims over his job and the invasion of his private life. Cameron decided against seeking legal advice from the company's lawyers in case it alerted them to potential problems. Notwithstanding that, Cameron did seek and obtained an increase in Barclay's offer, Barclay was unaware of the branch secretary's actions. Cameron handed the five-page document to Barclay advising that he could take the document away to consider it. Barclay ignored him and read the document. The first page contained the offer, the actual figures. The remaining pages related to confidentiality agreements to protect the business and of course him. Barclay read it quickly but comprehensively. One clause made Barclay pause and consider taking legal advice, or at least discussing it with the branch secretary. It related to Barclay not instigating any legal action against the company for any possible past breaches of company rules in that it would be unfair on the company not to have had the chance to resolve them through the internal grievance system.

The termination date was 30 September which was twenty-eight days from the coming Monday. Cameron insisted that it was a one-off offer which was not open to negotiation. He had until the Monday to sign or the offer would be withdrawn. Barclay said he would sign now. Cameron was relieved. He had already checked Barclay's leave record disclosing that he had some leave left. If he cleared his desk, handed over any outstanding work to the branch secretary, he could go at close of business the following day. The few days not covered by his annual leave would be considered gardening leave, and it would allow him to look for other employment if that was his intention.

In the afternoon after his own interview with Cameron, Bob Jardine asked Barclay about the restricted clauses. Yes, they were the same as in Barclay's offer. 'I'm not signing it. Are you?' He was shocked when Barclay said he had signed it. 'That's madness. They are obviously frightened of something with that clause about not taking legal action.'

'It's a one-off offer.'

'They're bluffing. Obviously they are hiding something. That's why they mention legal action. I'll tell them I'm not signing and they will come back with a better offer.' Barclay shrugged. Jardine insisted, 'I'm going to get some legal advice.'

Barclay thought about giving him the name of his employment lawyer, Mr Dougan, but knew that to do so would be merely mischievous.

The leaving party for the terminated staff was on 30 September in the local pub. Barclay decided to go. The branch secretary was leaving but not for another month. Cameron had realised that the restructuring needed a sure and efficient touch. Attention to detail was not Cameron's forte. Barclay was amused when told that Jardine had signed the agreement on the Monday morning. Jardine was more comfortable on the sidelines urging others to fight the system.

In response to Mr Payne's question, Barclay said his health was fine. On the Monday of that week he had received a telephone call from Gartnavel Royal Hospital informing him that an appointment was available the next morning due to a cancellation. Yes he would attend.

He did attend, nevertheless, he felt the psychiatrist had been desultory in his approach, not demonstrating the same interest or probing his personal history as much as his GP. Barclay was sleeping better. His headaches and feelings of nausea had gone. He was controlling his drinking. The psychiatrist did not seem to link his feeling better to not working. Barclay had informed the psychiatrist that he was starting a part-time tutoring post at the university. The psychiatrist replied that it would not present a problem for Barclay, insisting that academics have an easy, stress-free life. There was no need to put him on medication. He would review him in six months. If Barclay felt he was slipping back, then he was to contact the psychiatrist's secretary and she would arrange an appointment. The psychiatrist provided his card with the necessary telephone numbers.

University Tutor

Barclay had been looking for a job during his gardening leave. Acting on Mr Payne's advice, he went to Glasgow University to enquire about doing a PhD. He recognised two of the administration staff in the English department office especially the older woman who was the undergraduate coordinator or something. Neither recognised him.

'Ian Barclay?' asked the man at the back of the office.

'Yes.' He did not recognise the man dressed smartly in jacket and tie.

'Douglas Lennox.' A smile. 'You don't recognise me. I was the hippie lecturer.' Barclay recalled the young, long-haired lecturer normally dressed in denim. 'I'm the head of department now.' His splayed hands moved down to his waist. 'Hence the conservative dress. I'm part of the establishment.' He came forward to the counter which protected the sanctity of the office from students. 'You should have got a First.' Barclay sighed and the older secretary looked up from her desk at Barclay, a hint of recognition. 'You were cheated out of it if I remember.' Disapproval on the older woman's face. 'Let's go to my office for a chat.'

Barclay gave him a truncated history since graduating. He had left teaching because he found teaching the first and second years boring and unrewarding. Lennox was under-standing, stating that he could not have taught in secondary school. In response to leaving insurance with a package because of 'restructuring', the other man was sympathetic. 'Bloody Thatcher. That woman is destroying our industries and whole communities. We'll be next. There will be edicts on what we can and cannot teach.' Allowing Lennox's tirade to recede, Barclay told him that he was enquiring about doing a PhD. 'Ian, I wouldn't bother. I think you would be wasting your money. You wouldn't get a grant. Might get some funding from trusts, foundations, organisations like that.' He paused to allow Barclay to take it in and ask questions. None came. 'And the chances of getting a teaching post here would be slim. Politics. Our masters are keen to recruit people from Oxbridge. They think people with Oxbridge degrees even American ones from Harvard or Yale will attract students especially from overseas. Soon there will be no grants, well, very little.'

'I see.' Disappointment in his voice.

'But there might be another way. Can you survive for a while without a regular salary or with a small one, a very small one?'

'Yes. That's why I thought about the PhD. Got my pay-off and already have some savings... and my mortgage is reasonably low.'

'Lucky bloody you!' Lennox held up his right hand, palm open. 'I apologise. Not the language expected of the Professor of English at this ancient and renowned University.' He smiled. 'My degree is from an even more ancient and renowned university to the east.'

'Edinburgh?'

'*Certainly* not! That's a young university. The ancient and august Saint Andrews. Even here came before Edinburgh.'

'Oh, I didn't know that.'

'And a MLitt from Cambridge. So I ticked all the right

boxes despite my long hair and denim shirt. They probably put it down to a passing, youthful, rebellious phase. They were right. It is wise to bend with the wind especially when a chair is on offer.' Another smile, laced with vanity. 'Anyway, about you. Sometimes we need tutors for the first and second years. We use the PhDs and some of our retired lecturers. I'm sure I could persuade the department to use you.' Then, an impish smile. 'I know I can. I am the head of department.'

Barclay laughed, relaxing and remembering the young lecturer not staid like the others, full of jokes. Someone had likened him to Billy Connolly, the Glasgow comedian then making his name. Although he did recall that both Bernie and Peter did not care for him, Lennox not Connolly. Both thought Lennox was superficial, full of bluff and bluster. His attention and teaching directed at the frivolous, female students. A fraud. He would not mention that. Time to bend with the wind.

'Are you interested?'

'Yes.'

'It would only be about six hours a week to begin with. Spread over two or three days. The rate is fixed and you will be paid only for the actual tutorial hours. So don't spend hours preparing. Preparation time is included in the rate. Also, you will be paid for marking essays. You don't have to.'

'That's not a problem. What will I be teaching?'

'Straight to the important part. From what I recall, Ian Barclay did not waste time on pleasantries. Anyway. The essential matters. It's *King Lear* and *Paradise Lost... Book Four*. Should be no problem for you.'

'*Lear* is not a problem. Little bit rusty on Milton.'

'Sure your rustiness will be ten times more knowledgeable than the students.'

'I will dig out my notes. I have still got all my university ones.' Feeling slightly embarrassed at this disclosure

'Tutorials are slightly different now. Not so free ranging. There are set questions and issues for each tutorial.'

Barclay was a little surprised but it would help him.

'Once you get started and the students like them, sure we'll be able to add some more hours – maybe a couple of lectures.'

'That would be good. I'm already looking forward to it. When do I start?'

'Term starts in two weeks and the tutorials begin two weeks after. The contract is for a term only. We need to look at the finances before each term to make sure we have enough money to pay the part-time tutors. Is that acceptable?'

'Yes.'

'Good. Some forms to be done. Contact, bank details and so on. I'll take you back round to the office and you can do the admin.'

'Right. Good.'

'Just one more thing, Ian. Students are a bit different from your time. More demanding. Quick to complain. They are no longer empty vessels, more hissing kettles.'

His mother died and she was cremated in the first week of October.

Elaine had made all the arrangements by telephone initially before she arrived in Glasgow. Elaine did not even ask him to help with the arrangements for the funeral. Barclay was upset also guilty that he had not visited his mother as often as he should have done. At the purvey after the service, he felt hostility from Elaine's husband and even her two boys. The hostility was because all their gran had talked about was

Ian, and often she had expressed the hope that they, her two grandsons, would grow up to get good jobs like their Uncle Ian.

His sister told him that he should return to London and was confident that he could get a job there. Why didn't he approach his London college? Was the part-time enough? From London he could travel to Europe quicker and cheaper. She knew he enjoyed those trips well, guessed he did because he would rather go to Europe than come up to see his mother. He was angered. 'That's not fair.'

Elaine did not respond. Her brother had been cosseted throughout his life but never appreciated, or probably never realised what others did or tried to do for him. Apart from family, she thought of Peter Mayne, the posh, handsome English boy, who for some unfathomable reason took under his wing an awkward, meek Glasgow student.

It was Utopia.

He had returned to his university as a tutor not as he had once hoped as a lecturer. That was the past which he would not dwell on.

His first tutorials were with the first year undergraduates. Most were girls but they were all enthusiastic and willing to learn. The gloom returned on encountering his second year students. The girls were sullen and hostile, the boys uninterested and disengaged apart from a keen student from Portsmouth who reminded Barclay of Peter Mayne, the same easy charm but much brighter. Unlike Peter, the girls were not attracted to the Portsmouth student, and were openly antagonistic towards him.

The first complaint was that he did not explain the difficult language of Milton's text and concentrated only on the tutorial questions. Barclay acknowledged there was much to cover in so few tutorials. He sensed, knew that most of the second years had not read the text or prepared for the tutorials.

'They find the language difficult,' said Professor Lennox.

'It is university. It's not supposed to be easy. Surely the lectures are where the language should be discussed.'

'I know. But I think you need to have a little more come and go with them, especially the girls.'

'Right, Professor.' Barclay stood up.

'Ian, I told you we all use first names in the department. It's a different and more modern world from your day.'

'Right. Thanks… Douglas.' He was hesitant and un-comfortable.

There followed another few complaints from the second years. The final one was about his marking of the class essay.

'Some of them think you were a bit harsh in your marking. The extract was too long and rather difficult.'

'I didn't set the question. Anyway in the extract about the introduction of Adam and Eve, the language becomes simpler and plainer. There are almost no classical allusions.'

'Yes, Ian, I know. Nevertheless, take Julie's essay.' He picked up the essay, flicked through the pages and read from the marking sheet, 'The use of paradox and the matter of the word order is so important in Milton and should have received more attention.' He paused, looked up at Ian and smiled. 'A tad harsh?'

'No, I don't think so. As you know, they *are* important in Milton, and need to be addressed. Anyway, she still gained a good grade.'

'Yes, yes. Julie is in my tutorial group... and she's a bit of a star.' Barclay knew that his tutorials were on the novel, the easiest part of the course. Lennox put down Julie's essay and picked up another one. 'In this one... Gina's... you note that 'Dishevelled' and 'wanton' are pejorative terms and you say she should have said what they suggest about Eve. Then you give the answer to say that they suggest a flaw in Eve which the serpent will exploit.' He looked at Ian. 'Do you think a young girl could make these connections?'

'Yes!' He realised he had been abrupt and softened his tone. 'I would have expected most of these points to have been covered in the lectures.'

'Yes, yes. You're right, Ian.'

'Surely here in university, we should be challenging them to think beyond their years and maturity.' He knew he was borrowing Mr Baxter's words, his English teacher in his fourth year of secondary school.

'Of course, naturally. But some of the students, most of them, are not of the same quality as you.' He smiled in-gratiatingly. 'Do you want to review them? Adjust some of the marks possibly... or are you satisfied...'

'Yes. I spent quite some time marking and reviewing them. I am satisfied the marks are right and fair.'

'Of course, Ian.' He stood up. 'Thanks for coming in to see me.' The smile remained present till Barclay had left the room.

The final tutorial before the Christmas holidays was a revision session for the examinations in January. Barclay told the students that he had not and would not see the exam paper, and therefore, he could not give any clues. However, he covered the salient points and advised that they reread the observations and extensive notes, which he had made on their essays. Although the extract from the class essay would not be in the exam, there would still be links and most of the same points would apply. The second year students were receptive and made copious notes. He desisted from saying they should have been making such notes in the previous tutorials. Most of his tutorial group including Julie and Gina wished him a Merry Christmas. The Portsmouth boy stayed behind to thank him and hoped that he would be in Barclay's tutor group next term.

Barclay like the other temporary tutors were told to telephone the undergraduate office in the second week of January to confirm if they were still needed for the next term and to arrange a time to attend to sign their contracts. Barclay duly telephoned and was told to come in the following day just before mid-day. An hour or so after this telephone call, he received another from the undergraduate's office.

'Is that Mister Barclay?' He thought it was the older secretary's voice.

'Yes.'

'I'm sorry Mister Barclay. There has been a mistake. You are not required for the coming term.'

'Oh. May I ask why?'

'Yes... eh... well due to timetable changes...' He thought he could hear another voice, a male voice passing instructions. He knew it was Lennox. 'Some of the permanent staff are now available to take some of the tutorials.'

'Oh, I see. That's disappointing... I was so looking forward to coming back. I really enjoyed tutoring.'

'Yes, I understand. Excuse me a moment.' She seemed to be speaking to someone else. 'Mister Barclay, are you still there?'

'Yes.'

' I am really sorry. The students liked you.' She was speaking freely. 'The business with the class essay was unfortunate.

I am glad you did not change the marks.' She did not tell him that Douglas Lennox had changed some of the marks. 'Maybe you could try Strathclyde? Probably too late for this term. Anyway, I think they do semesters'

'Yes. Thanks.'

'I do remember you. You were friends with Peter Mayne and the two Irish girls?'

'Yes.'

'One… can't remember her name… was murdered.'

'Yes. Christine.'

'Terrible, terrible.'

Why did she have to mention it, thought Barclay.

The older secretary did not reveal that Christine was due to attend for an interview a week or so after she had been murdered. Barclay did not seem all that interested or shocked by her death.

'I need to go… and I'm sorry again.'

'Thanks.'

Recess: The Ending

25 January. Burns Day.

He decided to celebrate early. A drink or two before lunch. He drank quickly half of the full glass of wine.

Scotland's greatest bard! Huh! Burns and Scott, *sham bards of a sham nation*, according to Edwin Muir in his poem *Scotland 1941*. Apart from *Tam O'Shanter*, he did not like the Ayrshire man's poetry, never being able to get to grips with it. As indeed he had been unable to fully grasp much of Scottish literature, no actual intercourse, apart from Muriel Spark whom he did not consider a Scottish writer simply a writer who should have a place within the pantheon of the literary greats. Of course, he had read the novels of other Scottish writers, liking Eric Linklater's *Magnus Merriman*, Iain Crichton Smith's writings and James Kennaway's *Tunes of Glory*. The tough, fighting soldier Jock Sinclair from Glasgow had been betrayed by his closest comrade. Despite the actor being English, he had enjoyed Alec Guinness's portrayal of Jock in the film. But the betrayal of Jock had angered him, and had he not tried to hold Major Charlie Scott to account.

The bottle of Sauvignon Blanc was empty.

His anger was a sham. Barclay knew his real sympathy, his affinity was with the effete, Eton and Oxford educated Barrow whom Sinclair cruelly mocked as Barrow Boy. In the film, Barrow had been played by John Mills, and both the character and actor reminded him of his decent, friendly, cerebral colleagues at the sixth-form college in London. Also like him, Barrow had been a prisoner. Barclay told himself he still was. In the same way as Barrow he was ill-at ease with others. His life had been controlled and dictated by others. It was Peter Mayne, he thought, who told him not to be a *wee, sleekit, cowran, tim'rous beastie*. Probably the only words of Burns which the refined Peter knew. Barclay had to stand up for himself. Bernie had told him the same. He had been cheated out of a first-class honours degree at Glasgow University, the Yoonie. While he knew from Cairns' legal training, there was no relevant or sufficient evidence to support a conviction on that charge.

Whisky was mandatory in order to properly honour Burns and not by imbibing cheap wine .

Once the necessary changes had been completed, he sat down again in his chair. Or was that his prison, his place of confinement!?

The first of the whisky.

Peter, Bernie and Christine had been his only true and loyal friends. Yes, he acknowledged that Mr Yates, the college principal, and Mr Payne, the branch secretary, had helped and advised him but that was their duty, their obligation.

More whisky.

He wondered where Peter was. Had he really joined the army? Possibly, he was serving in Northern Ireland. Many soldiers were, and he would hear in the morning news, 'Last night, another soldier…'

Bernie, the ever joyful and impish Bernadette – he had preferred the latter name but one did not argue with Bernie. She was no doubt still teaching in the school in… He could not remember the name of the town. Magherafelt? Yes, it was

Magherafelt with Mary's, the 'best wee pub in the world'. And no doubt Bernie was very popular with her pupils. A chuckle. Did she have a Bernie set? Her favoured pupils? Did she tell of her life in Glasgow, at the Yoonie. Did she talk of Ian Barclay and Peter Mayne, the latter who said more than his prayers. Another chuckle. He had not heard the expression in a long time. Last time was probably when used by that cold Go… Goaden… he couldn't remember his name. He knew that not remembering was becoming more frequent. Anyway, where would he be now had he become a civil servant?

A sip of whisky.

No! Bernie would not have a set. He smiled. She would not favour one pupil over another. She would not discriminate. She argued with anyone. His smile faded. She would not have approved of Jean Brodie. A vague memory seeped into his mind. They had been discussing the novel, or had they gone to see the film. Didn't matter. Bernie had declared that Miss Jean Brodie was a terrible teacher and should not be allowed anywhere near children. Peter, of course, had made some off-colour comment of her being allowed near him which was probably aimed more at Maggie Smith, the actress who played the title role. Barclay had not liked Smith's performance or the film because it did not keep true to the words of the novel. His Higher English teacher, not Mr Baxter, had stressed the need to concentrate on the actual words of a text. Good acting of course was essential to convey the text's message but overacting could undermine even erode the message. It was more difficult when a novel was transformed into a film because always there had to be additional dialogue.

He recalled the last time he had met Bernie on Gilmore Hill. She had invited him over to Ireland. He was too fearful to go there. He wondered if she ever saw Christine… no, no… Christine is dead. The only girl he had ever loved.

Shot down, murdered on the street by loyalists – her only crime being trying to end discrimination against Catholics – and she was a Protestant. Tears infiltrated his eyes.

More whisky to ease the grief.

On his return from the bathroom, he went to the window looking down at the almost deserted street. It was near to mid-day. Most people would be at work or school. A boy and a girl, students no doubt, were walking hand-in-hand towards Clarence Drive, one of the two main roads through Hyndland from where one could catch a bus. He felt envy towards them: it only accentuated his loneliness. Then the thought. If Peter is in Ireland, maybe he has met Bernie. He always had a thing for her. Possibly they are married. No. She did not love him.

He was digressing. Keep to what is relevant and specific. What if Bernie is right? Then Sandy was right to put a stop to Miss Brodie. Sandy was innocent. Miss Jean Brodie is guilty!

He sat striving to unclutter his mind. There was no need for this constant analysis: an infection caused by a love of literature. Love causes hurt, it is claimed, but, not the deep and intense pain inflicted by the lack of love. He closed his eyes. He should rest. No! He knew what he would do. He would go back to Vienna to seek out Irmelin. He would go to the bar… the wonder… wunder… in Schultegasse, Schuster… no that was not the name… but he knew he could find it. Even if she was not there, people would not have forgotten the beautiful, blonde-haired girl. Yes, that's what he would do. Almost immediately, he shouted, 'You fool, Barclay! She's not there.' He remembered she had been going to London to marry. How would he find her there? People in London who met her would not forget the strikingly beautiful, blonde-haired

Austrian girl, woman now. But her husband, he could be a problem and object to this Glaswegian like Lochinvar turning up to claim his woman. He was likely to be a blond-haired, muscular, Austrian giant. Nevertheless, he would embark on his quest.

First, he would make a sandwich for his lunch. A foray into the kitchen to make and eat a ham and tomato sandwich, a 'piece' as it was called when he was growing up. He had not brought his whisky into the kitchen so instead had a glass of water.

He had been a tenant too long. He would announce to the world his rejection of *the old dispensation* and his rebirth.

The two doors were locked, having not followed his morning routine of opening the inner door then unlocking the storm door. He opened the inner or vestibule door and stepped into the small vestibule. The noise was loud as the bunch of keys escaped from his hand and struck the stone floor. He shook his head, alarmed that the noise might disturb any neighbours not at work. It took effort in bending down to retrieve the keys, almost falling back into his hallway. Finally, he managed to pull himself up and unlocked the double storm doors. Leaving both the inner and outer doors wide open, he stepped gingerly onto the landing. On leaving his flat, the stairs were immediately to his left, then the right-angled wooden banister, more a balustrade with Greco-Roman type spars running its length from the half-landing up turning left to end at the wall of the neighbouring flat. He was pleased that his immediate neighbour's double door was closed. He did not know this neighbour, hardly saw him and when he did, merely exchanged polite nods.

His hands gripping the polished, brown, wooden banister and looking down at the half-landing he proclaimed. '*Friends,*

Romans, Countrymen…' He shook his head mumbling, 'No, no, not Anthony… Brutus'

'As Caesar loved me, I weep for him; as he was fortunate, I rejoice in… him… no… it ; as he was valiant… I honour… but, as he was ambitious, I slew him.' He was swaying needing the stability of the banister. He continued, *'Not that I loved Caesar less, but that I love Rome more…* no, the order was wrong… that part came first… maybe not… But, I want to… renounce the past.'

He noticed two boys in their green school jackets had joined the crowd on the half-landing below. They would be frightened, anxious, which was natural being amongst a volatile crowd after a foul and bloody murder.

Miss Boyd was there. *'Mister* Barclay. What are you doing?' She had come down from the flat above hearing the noise. 'You are terrifying Tony Cairns' boys.' Barclay had slumped down onto the top step leaning against the banister. She shepherded the two boys up the stairs past Barclay and told them to ask their mother to telephone for an ambulance.

Barclay became agitated. 'It's not fair! Why fucking me!' Miss Boyd undeterred and not intimidated told him to stop shouting and swearing.

Another neighbour had telephoned the police.

Barclay was drowsy trying to keep his eyes open. He was aware of the two policemen on the half-landing looking up at him. Miss Boyd asked them to wait. It was probably a medical problem. Mrs Cairns had shouted down confirming she had telephoned for an ambulance

'Why? Mum left me. I'm sorry Mum… I'm so sorry… I know. Veronica. Why?' Tears now wetting his face. 'Christine… I loved you only you… Why? Who did it?' He wiped his eyes with the back of his right hand. 'Peter deserted me.'

He looked up. 'He probably deserted the army!' He was hysterical, clutching the thick spar on the landing which formed the right angle.

He intoned, '*Now, Lycidas, the shepherds weep no more.*' Despairingly he shouted, 'The shepherds will not weep for me.' He shook his head. He recalled Jock Sinclair's explanation of a pibroch being a lament, trying to recall the exact description: *It's no just a grieving... something angry about it.* Barclay knew through the tears that he was a pibroch, a coalescence of grief and anger, lamenting the cost and futility of his love of literature. He had been a tenant in a cul-de-sac, looking at the same buildings.

Two ambulance men were coming up the stairs. One was trying to reassure him, 'It's alright now, sir.' The other getting his name from Miss Boyd. 'Ian. We're here to help you. We'll get you down into the ambulance.' Miss Boyd was telling Barclay that she would lock up and safeguard his keys. They confirmed to her that they would be going straight to Gartnavel Royal Hospital. He was being lifted up but gently by the four uniformed men, boxed in, still caged like the Duchess of Malfi.

Eliot's line from *Journey of the Magi* came into his head: *I should be glad of another death.*

Now after all those years, Barclay understood its meaning.

Acknowledgments

I thank Peter Howe for his advice and guidance on the language and structure. Where I have not followed his advice, was not due to its quality but to my obstinacy. I wish to express my thanks to Gerard McManus and Roísín Ritchie for their suggestions and positive encouragement. The latter and I share different views of 'Ian Barclay'.

Thanks also to Claire Adams for her work on the cover, Man Suk Yee for her drawings and to Duncan Lockerbie of Lumphanan Press for his help in bringing *The Wrackful Tenancy* to publication.